ECHO OF A
STUART

Recent Titles by Elizabeth Elgin from Severn House

FOOTSTEPS OF A STUART

WHISPERS ON THE WIND

ECHO OF A STUART

Elizabeth Elgin

This edition first published in Great Britain 1998 by
SEVERN HOUSE PUBLISHERS LTD of
9–15 High Street, Sutton, Surrey SM1 1DF.
Originally published in 1973 in Great Britain by
Robert Hale Ltd. under the pseudonym Kate *Kirby*.
This title first published in the USA 1998 by
SEVERN HOUSE PUBLISHERS INC., of
595 Madison Avenue, New York, NY 10022.

British Library Cataloguing in Publication Data

Elgin, Elizabeth
        Echo of a Stuart
        1.   Great Britain - History - Elizabeth, 1558-1603 - Fiction
        2.   Historical fiction
        1.   Title
        823.9'14 [F]

        ISBN 0-7278-2208-X

Printed and bound in Great Britain by
MPG Books Ltd, Bodmin, Cornwall.

PART ONE

1586

CHAPTER ONE

THE man who stood in the shadows by Weaver's Oak damned the cold March evening. He had waited since dusk and he was chilled and hungry and not a little anxious. This was the third night he had kept vigil by the crossroads; surely soon the carpenter must arrive?

A white owl ghosted above him, beating the air with noiseless wings, hooting as it hunted to scare into movement the small creatures upon which it preyed. And so still was the man in the shadows that the great nightbird almost brushed his face as it glided past him.

"Mother of God, is this game worth it?" he asked silently. "Only a fool would stand half perished with cold and hunger. And you, Cedric Woodhall," he thought, "are a fool!"

His mouth quirked downward in derision. It amazed him that so complete was the lie he lived, so perfect the deception, that now even he imagined himself to be Cedric Woodhall. How long since he had used his rightful name? How soon before he could use it again and claim what was his own? How soon before Elizabeth Tudor rotted stinking in her grave? was the answer he gave himself.

Nothing had changed in Aldbridge, thought the man. The manor house still watched over the green; the mill-wheel still turned where the beck curved in a long

slow loop and the inn by St. Olave's church was noisy
and dirty as ever. Once, and only once since he had left
it, he had walked through the village, *his* village. It had
been a foolhardy thing to do and until the time was
right he must never do it again.

Here, where the Ripon road ran straight into York
and was crossed by the track that wound through the
forest to Knaresborough was the nearest he now dared
venture to Aldbridge. Here, at these God-forsaken crossroads where night birds hunted and men still remembered the ways of the old religion and blessed themselves
as they hurried past, was where he must wait.

Until they had killed Elizabeth Tudor, that was.

A footstep caused him to start forward. Master Owen?
He opened his mouth to frame the question then held
his breath and melted once more into the shadows. Some
fool who would have done better to sit by his hearth and
pile logs into the blaze had almost made him betray his
presence. Some fool, who, if his hurrying footsteps were
anything to go by, would soon no doubt, be doing just
that.

Had he, thought Woodall, missed the carpenter? *The
crossroads above Aldbridge village,* the message had
instructed. Surely there had not been a change of plan?
It was as well his wife did not question his comings and
goings. Some women would be curious, might even
demand to know what strange business took her man
from his home at all hours of the day and night. But not
so with Jane, his wife. He could be gone for a week, and
only a lifting of her eyebrows would acknowledge his
return.

Damn her indifference! Were it not for pretty little Beth, he swore he'd have sent the shrewish bitch on her way long ago. But now it suited him to have a woman who asked no questions. He had wed her in Elizabeth Tudor's church with the blessing of a heretic priest and it pleased his conscience that by God's Holy laws it was not a valid marriage. When the time came it would be easy enough to be rid of her.

The trundling wooden wheels scratched slowly to a halt and in the darkness a man coughed. Cedric Woodhall reached for a twig and snapped it in his hands. Nearby a man coughed again.

"Well met, friend," Woodhall stepped forward.

A small, fair-haired man turned, his eyes searching the blackness for the owner of the voice.

"It is a cold night, for March," he replied.

"It will be less cold in Douai."

The stranger set down the legs of the little cart he pushed and held out his hand.

"I am glad to meet you, sir. Have you waited long?"

"I wait as long as I must," Woodhall replied with a shrug. The man had relaxed when the word *Douai* had been mentioned. Surely now the long wait was over?

"You are Nicholas Owen?" he asked.

Sharply the stranger lifted his head.

"Sir," he replied, "I do not ask your name and I pray you do not ask mine. Some men know me as Master Andrews, others call me John Draper, and some have dubbed me Little John of the Little Beard; but Nicholas Owen I cannot own."

A*   9

"Your pardon, Master Andrews, but I right glad am to see you. I will not be so careless again."

"Thank you, good friend." The gentle face creased into a smile. "Soon, if God wills it, there will be an end to this subterfuge and we will all be as careless and carefree as we would wish. And now, what news have you?"

"Bad news, I fear." Cedric Woodhall dropped his voice. "I was to take you to my house in York and there you were to wait further orders. But York seethes with Walsingham's Protestant spies. They are on every street corner and in every inn. There is much sympathy for Mistress Clitheroe. The Council are bent on having her life and the citizens of York would need little prodding to rise up in protest on her behalf. Know you, Master Andrews, that she is to be brought before the Council of the North on a charge of harbouring Catholic priests?"

The fair-haired man nodded.

"Aye, I have heard it. And I will pray for the brave woman. But surely they will not have her life? They say she is with child."

"It will make no difference. They did not take the priest they sought, but there was evidence in her house that Mass had been said there. And she will not help herself. She refused to plead. She says she has committed no sin against God."

"Then she is even braver than I thought," Master Andrews thoughtfully stroked his beard, "for if she will not plead her death will be the more savage. And death awaits us all if we do not tread carefully."

"It is God's Will," Cedric Woodhall answered with an indifference he did not feel.

He did not want to die. He had been near to death almost twenty years ago, and the memory of it still made his stomach churn. He wondered if men who talked so glibly of death had smelled its sickening stench.

Twenty years ago he had been little more than a youngling. He had known neither pain nor hunger and the world had been his kicking-ball, or so he had thought. And when the Black Angel of death had crooked a finger at him he had been glad enough to bargain for his life. Now, for the sake of his Catholic conscience, he played a double game, and if he were discovered there would be no second chance.

"You are to go to Weston Hall. It is the house of Sir Malger de Vavasour and the Lady Johan." Cedric Woodhall was eager to be rid of his thoughts. "They will give you shelter and doubtless will find you work until I can reach you again."

"Aye, Sir Melger is a good Catholic. No doubt there will be some part of his home I can put to good use before I leave."

He nodded his head. He knew the house, distantly. It was old and rambling, and there would be many nooks and corners that could be disguised, with his help, to hide a hunted priest.

"If you will point me on my way, friend, I will detain you no longer."

"Weston lies to the south-west, but you cannot reach it this night. It would be better if you travelled to Staveley. There is a house by the church—you will know it by its twisted chimney stack. Mention Douai and you will be sure of shelter. From there you can travel to

Knaresborough in the morning. Weston is not far from there. You should make it in a day's journey."

"I thank you, sir."

The traveller held out his hand. Cedric Woodhall grasped the work-worn fingers in his.

"Take yonder track. About two miles ahead you will find a fork to the right hand. Staveley is little more than a mile away, then."

"And you, friend? How will you fare this night?"

Cedric Woodhall shrugged.

"I will take the road to York, and my own home. It is a fair step, but I have no cart to slow me down. With luck I shall make the city by daybreak. It will be easy to slip through Micklegate Bar with the tradesmen when they lift the portcullis. I shall not be noticed."

"Then God go with you, sir."

Cedric Woodhall stood by the oak tree and watched the man disappear into the night, pushing his cart before him. So slight a man, yet he would work as a carpenter by day in the house he visited, and at night would turn his hand to his other trade—that of building hiding holes for Catholic priests.

Always he worked alone, for none could be trusted to help him. His task was a labour of love and he did it humbly for God. The builder of priests' holes had already been imprisoned for his beliefs, but that had not deterred him. Cedric Woodhall had the grace to feel shame. But then, he reasoned, the carpenter had not lain under sentence of death or known the damp dark dungeons of London's Tower. And he was but a journeyman carpenter. He had no old score to settle nor had he been robbed of his inheritance.

Cedric Woodhall did not want to die. He wanted what was rightfully his, and that he would have when a Catholic prince sat once more on England's throne. So he would cheat and lie and deceive, and he would stay alive. Life owed him a great deal, and he, Cedric Woodhall, was not the stuff that martyrs are made of.

Let them take him and he would appeal to Sir Francis Walsingham. He had served Sir Francis well, and few men knew of his double dealings. Those who did, he reasoned, would face the rack rather than betray him. It suited him well to run with the hare and hunt with the hounds—that way he could not lose. And one day he would come back to Aldbridge!

The squeaking wheels of the little cart and the clang of the carpenter's gluepots were lost in the night.

"God go with *you*, Nicholas Owen," Cedric Woodhall said as he took the road to York.

The reluctant moon slipped behind a cloud and changed the beech trees that lined the green at Aldbridge and the squat square tower of St. Olave's church into indefinable ghostly shapes that well suited John Weaver's mood. His heart pounded loudly in his ears and his breath rasped sharply in his throat, for he had run almost a mile from the crossroads, and he was no longer a young man.

"Mother of Jesus, have mercy," he prayed as he headed for the safety of his home. "Saint Olave and all the Angels protect us!"

He pressed the lucky stone he held in his hand until

its jagged edges bit into his sweating palm, then gasped
with relief as the manor house loomed up before him,
four-square and solid, the lights from its mullioned
windows shining comfort, giving back his sanity.

Dropping the stone into the pocket of his jacket, he
placed his trembling hands on the trunk of the rowan
tree that grew beside his door. Safe at last he leaned his
burning cheek against its silk-cool bark, and gulped the
cold night air into his heaving lungs. Nothing now
could harm him, neither witch nor beastie, nor Lucifer
himself, for no evil thing dare venture near the all-
protecting rowan.

"Thanks be to God," he whispered, calmer now as he
lifted the iron latch on the heavy oak door. From the fireplace—that same fireplace Sir Crispin Wakeman before
him had finely rebuilt to burn the foul sea-coal—the
bright cheering blaze from the birch logs lighted the
great hall, touching the lofty smoke-blackened rafters
and dancing on the lovingly polished chairs and benches.

"Anne?" he questioned. "Anne, love?"

All would be well with Anne's calming hands in his.

"I am here, John."

From the open door of the cosy winter-parlour came
the dearly loved voice.

"You are early back from your walk. Your posset is not
ready yet."

Lady Anne Weaver laid aside the shirt she was sewing
and reached for the bell at her side.

"No Anne, not yet." John eased himself into a chair,
closing his eyes and letting the peace of the friendly little
room wash over him. "Not yet, love."

14

"John?"

In an instant she was by his side, kneeling at his feet, her hands reaching for his.

"What ails you, husband?" She laid a cooling hand on his forehead. "The ale at suppertime? Does it gripe your stomach?"

"No Anne, not the ale. My stomach churns, but it is not the ale."

"Then what—?"

Anne Weaver who knew her husband so completely, loved him so well, looked at the pale face above her and sensed fear.

For a while the only sound was the crackling of logs and the harsh, uneven breathing of the man who sat still and strangely alone by the hearth. Then, opening his eyes and swallowing loudly, he looked into the anxious face of his wife.

"This night, Anne, I saw the devil incarnate!"

"You saw the devil?"

John Weaver did not answer. Slowly he nodded his head.

"Then I'll swear it's more than the ale that churns your stomach." Anne Weaver sprang to her feet. "It is bed for you, husband, with a hot brick at your feet, for I fear you have caught a fever!"

She took his hands firmly in hers, seeking to draw him to his feet.

"The devil incarnate, indeed! And what form did this devil take? And where did you meet him, might I beg to ask?"

Wearily John turned his head against the disbelief in Anne's eyes.

"He stood in the shadows, I tell you. I saw him in a glance of moonlight, plain as I see you now." His eyes, unwavering, sought hers. "I saw him at Weaver's Oak."

"So!" Anne's mouth set in an obstinate line so familiar to her husband. "You've been to Meg's grave again? Cannot you let the little wench rest after all these years?"

"How can she rest?" Now John's fear was turning to anger. "How can the maid rest when Lucifer sends one to torment her?"

"And who did he send, John? Whose body did the devil take? Who stood by Meg's grave, do you imagine?"

"I did not imagine it Anne, and I did not imagine the white owl that flew around him. I saw him, I tell you, as plain as I see your beloved face. I saw Kit Wakeman at the crossroads!"

For a moment Anne Weaver was silent. She had hated Kit Wakeman with a venom that was foreign to her nature. Even now, after all the years, the sound of his name caused a tingle of distaste in her mouth.

"Kit Wakeman is dead! Master Christopher Wakeman got his just deserts a score years ago; and even the devil would not want him!"

"He stood there, I tell you."

"John love, listen to your Anne."

Gently she took his face between her hands, forcing him to look at her. She too was beginning to feel a little of her husband's fear, for John, Anne knew, was the most honest man that walked in shoe leather. In all their years

16

together, she had never known him to lie to her. Either he was sickening for a fever or he really believed he had seen Kit Wakeman.

"Listen to me," she coaxed, more gently. "Kit Wakeman, aye, even Lucifer himself and all his devils would not stand by Meg's grave. Did not Father Sedgwick give her absolution after death, and bless and sanctify the place where you had laid her? A devil would not stand on holy ground."

"I'll grant you he gave her absolution, Anne, but it was the least he could do. He refused the maid Christian burial."

Anne nodded.

"Aye, he did, and it tore at my heart. But he righted the wrong. Meg's sins were absolved I tell you. And her grave blessed."

"Father Sedgwick was a turn-coat priest," John countered stubbornly. "Kit Wakeman accused Meg of witchcraft, so she died without the blessing of the Church. Why did he call her a witch, Anne? Why must she lie buried at the crossroads?"

"It is a cross we must bear, and the good Lord sent young Harry to help us bear it."

"Would I had taken her body from that place and laid it decently to rest. I *could* have done it, Anne. When Queen Elizabeth gave me this manor and all its lands, none could have stopped me."

"No John, you could not, for all the Queen gave to you. You know it bodes ill to disturb the dead."

"Wherever they lie, Anne?"

"*Wherever!*"

17

"Then you think that Kit Wakeman can do Meg no wrong?"

"Kit Wakeman was evil, and he died evil. He is dead, John. *Dead!*"

And then the bitter look was gone from her face and she smiled lovingly at John.

"Did you not see his traitor's head stuck on a pole on London Bridge? Oh, John. Do you remember that time when Queen Elizabeth summoned you to London?" Anne was eager to wrest John's thoughts back to normality. "Do you remember how I fretted and thought I should never see you again?"

"Aye, love, I remember. And I remember the sweet disbelief on your face when I handed you the manor of Aldbridge on a plate, and gave you a fine lady's hat with a green plume in it."

"I often wonder why the Queen gave the manor and the title to you, John."

"There was none other to give it to, I think. Sir Crispin Wakeman had fled, outlawed for his part in the uprising against the Queen. Some man had to care for the poor starving souls of this village."

"You are too modest, John. The Queen gave it to you because you were a good man, and because you had been loyal to her cause during the uprising."

"Perhaps, Anne, she gave it to me to hold for Harry. Elizabeth Tudor knew about Meg's death and that Harry was Kit Wakeman's bastard. She knew in her youth the sting of that title. I think it gave the Queen strange pleasure to give to Meg's son what, by right of birth, should have gone to Kit Wakeman who fathered him and disowned him."

"And few know that Harry is not our son, and few know where Meg lies buried."

"Goody Trewitt knows all that. And Jeffrey, and Father Sedgwick."

"Father Sedgwick is long since dead, and Jeffrey loved Meg, so Harry's secret is safe with him. And as for Goody —she has not mentioned it from that day to this.

"Then only Kit Wakeman knows who Harry's true parents are."

"John Weaver!" Anne shook her head with impatience. "What in the name of all that's Holy am I to do with you? Kit Wakeman is dead. He knew of our deception. He knew that I had pretended to be with child so that we could spare Meg from shame. I tell you John, I thought with every passing day we would be found out, and Meg's condition plain for all to see. I'd not go through those months of lying and deceit again, not for two manors and their lands!"

"We could not have done it, but for Goody's help."

"We could not! She delivered Meg's babe, then found a wet-nurse for him when Meg died on the child bed. We have many true friends, John. Even Queen Elizabeth worded the title deed so that all these lands should pass to Harry. She made it plain that he was indeed our legitimate son. And who are we to gainsay what Elizabeth Tudor decrees?"

"Who indeed, my Lady Anne?"

John touched his wife's cheek with affection. She grew, he thought, more beautiful with each day that passed.

Sometimes he felt it was wrong to love someone as he loved Anne. And almost always Anne was right in what she said.

She was a down-to-earth woman of York and had accepted her new status with a dignity and humility that had amazed him. Overnight, almost, she had become the lady of the manor where once she had served Kit Wakeman's father, Sir Crispin, as a kitchen maid.

And still she was his Anne. Dear and sensible, loving and stubborn. Position and wealth had not changed her. Of course he must listen to what she said. Kit Wakeman was dead, and tonight, by the crossroads, it had been the trick of a fleeting shaft of moonlight that had deceived him.

Meg's poor grave had been blessed. He had planted an oak tree over it so that none could disturb her resting place. And that sapling oak had grown and flourished, and now men called it Weaver's Oak. That it had grown so strong was a good omen. Meg was safe from an army of devils—wasn't she?

The little serving maid answered Anne's ringing bell.

"Take hot bricks from inside the fire-oven, Molly, and lay them in Sir John's bed. The master has a slight ague and needs the warmth."

"And Sir John's posset, my lady?"

"I will make it myself. Do as I bid you, and then be off to your rest."

"I thank you." The girl bobbed a curtsey. "Goodnight my lady. The angels guard you."

Anne nodded.

"The angels guard *you*, Molly," she said.

Carefully as she stood by the fireplace in the lofty kitchen —the kitchen she had known so well as a girl—Anne Weaver measured a spoonful of Goody Trewitt's sleeping draught and stirred it into the posset she prepared.

How often had she damned Kit Wakeman? How often, long ago, had she thought "The devil take you, Kit Wakeman"? How bitterly had she said it? And had the devil taken her at her word? Had John really seen that evil youngling standing by Meg's grave? Kit Wakeman had had Meg's body. Had he now come back for her soul?

Well, he should not have it! Devil or no devil, she would settle Kit Wakeman's hash, once and for all! She would find her rosary. Once, she had been a good Catholic. Now she prayed in Elizabeth Tudor's church, for she firmly believed there was but one God and one Hereafter. She had once served Kit Wakeman's family who had never accepted King Henry's church or his divorce from Queen Catherine.

Sir Crispin Wakeman had risen up in support of Mary Stuart, the Queen of Scotland whom all Catholics believed should be Queen of England, too. And because Meg had learned of the plot to seize Elizabeth Tudor's throne, she had been denounced as a witch to silence her. If the Catholics had not rebelled all those years ago, Meg would be alive now.

Those thoughts had helped Anne to forget the teachings of the old religion and accept the new one, but Kit Wakeman had died a Catholic, and maybe, if the good God frowned on Elizabeth Tudor's church, perhaps it would be as well to put things to rights. Perhaps Meg's absolution from an Anglican priest was not acceptable to God?

Tomorrow, at daybreak, over Meg's grave, Anne would say her rosary as she had done as a girl, and then she would bury it beneath Weaver's Oak. Meg would be safe then, and Kit Wakeman would never have her soul.

"Damn you, Master Wakeman," she muttered as she furiously stirred her posset. "Damn you into all Eternity!"

CHAPTER TWO

JOHN WEAVER had slept late and awakened refreshed. Now in the fine bright light of the spring morning, the events of the previous evening seemed to have lost some of their horror.

Anne had risen early and returned with the early dew on her slippers. How like Anne to painstakingly gather herbs in readiness for the Easter Day feast, thought John, though why she should pick them from the hedgerows when she had a herb-garden full of them he did not understand. But always, Anne had her reasons.

By the gate of the corn-mill, Jeffrey Miller raised his hand in salute as John approached, then settled himself comfortably on his elbows to wait, a broad smile of welcome spreading across his open honest face.

"Bid you good morning, Sir John!"

Sir John Weaver and Jeffrey the Miller had a special relationship steel-bonded by their memories of Meg, but still Jeffrey gave John his rightful due and never failed to tip his cap or his forelock in greeting.

"Well met, Jeffrey. This is a fine morning and I come to ask a favour."

"It is yours, Sir John, if I can grant it."

"Young Diccon? I hear he is home again?"

Jeffrey grinned.

"Aye, the young ruffian is home and away to Skelton to

my brother's farm, full of tales about Drake and the Spanish Main, and eager to take up where he left off, I don't doubt, with my brother's dairy maid! "

Jeffrey rubbed the back of his neck ruefully.

"The sooner the little wench catches him, the sooner I'm hoping he'll forget his sea-faring and settle down here at the mill."

"And when will he return, Jeffrey?"

"By the morning, on strictest instructions from his mother."

"Then perhaps you could spare him for yet another day? My men are busy sowing in the fields, and young Harry comes home from school on Thursday for his Easter holidays. I'd be mighty grateful if Diccon could ride to York with a horse for him."

"He'd like that fine, Sir John. He and Master Harry are rare friends, and it will give him the chance to have a look at the city."

"York city will seem like a village market to Diccon after all the sights he has seen. Why did he go to sea, do you fancy?"

"Nay, I declare I'll never know, but a lad must get the wildness out of his blood, and to sail with Sir Francis Drake is one of the best ways I know of doing it."

"You never farmed the land at Skelton, Jeffrey. Your uncle willed it to you, yet you left farming and worked your father's mill. How so?"

"I always had a mind when the farm came to me to take Meg there, but it was not to be. Now my brother rents it from me—it matters little to me now."

"You still talk of Meg, Jeffrey, yet you have a good and

loving wife, and five fine sons to prove it. Do you remember her still, as I do?

"Aye, Sir John. I could not forget Meg. Once, we were pledged and I came home to Aldbridge with a length of silk and a wedding ring in my pack, but it was not to be. Instead I found her battered and bleeding at the hands of a witch-hunting mob, and big with Kit Wakeman's child."

"And still you wanted to marry Meg, for all that?"

"Aye, still I wanted her. And when the blossom is on the trees and the first heartsease lifts its tiny face, I am a youngling again, and Meg sits by the beck, weaving fantasies. And my loins ache from wanting her, as though it were but yesterday."

"How does your wife, friend?"

Jeffrey grinned.

"There'll be the devil to pay if this babe she carries is not a girl. My Judith has a great longing for a little maid to pet and spoil. Make no mistake Sir John," he hastened, "I have a good wife and I am grateful for it. Only to have known Meg is to love her for all time."

"Do you know where Meg lies buried, Jeffrey?"

"I have my thoughts, Sir John, as have most of the village, but if you wished it to be known you would have told us long since."

"Aye."

John hesitated. He had been on the point of telling Jeffrey about his encounter of the previous evening, but now with the daffodils nodding and the apple trees bursting their fat pink buds, it seemed neither the time

25

nor the place. The day was too sweet to talk of Kit Wakeman.

"Then I'll be on my way to Mistress Trewitt's. Lady Anne has sent bread for her and I am packed off with it like an errand boy," laughed John. "We'll expect Diccon bright and early on Thursday, then?"

"Bright and early," promised Jeffrey Miller.

The fire in Goody Trewitt's hearth puffed smoke as John opened her door.

"Shut that door, John Weaver, do," grumbled the old woman as she sat by the hearth. "These logs are damp and smoky enough without you making things worse."

"Then I'll carry in some wood for you, and set it by the hearth to dry. You should not live alone, Goody. Often my Anne says it. There's bed and board for you at the manor house whenever you want it. Will you not come to live with us? You are our oldest and dearest friend and Anne worries about you, especially in the winter time."

"I'll come when I'm good and ready, John Weaver," snapped the old woman. "What's in yon basket you carry?"

" 'Tis fresh-baked bread and some of Anne's cheese— if you can eat it, that is."

"Away with your teasing, John Weaver. I'm an old woman and the only pleasure left to me is my belly. Lord, how I stand these fish-days of Lent I'll never know. There wouldn't be a chicken leg in the basket would there?"

"There would not, Goody Trewitt, and you are a wicked old woman to think that Anne would break the

Lenten feast—even for you!"

Goody drew back the fine white cloth that covered the basket.

"My, but she's a wonderful cook is your Anne. I shall enjoy this breakfast."

"Anne did not bake the bread, Goody. Agnes Muff does most of the cooking at the manor, and well you know it. Anne cannot spend as much time in the kitchen as she would like with the village to tend."

"Aye, Fat Agnes has a fine hand with victuals, but there'll never be a cook like your Anne. I remember the day—'twas before you left the farm, John, when Anne brought home her new fire-oven. My, how she worked to get it! I think that fire-oven pleased her more than all the great kitchens at the manor house will ever do."

John Weaver was silent. He remembered the day well. Walter Skelton, the travelling weaver had arrived that same night. Meg had been alive then, and now Walter, friend of his youth had gone. Deliberately John closed down his thoughts.

"You'll be with us for the Easter Feast, Goody? There's a lamb and two fine geese hanging in the dairy, and there'll be apple pies and syllabub, and old barley wine to wash it down with. Can you stir your old bones to pay us a call on Sunday, do you think?"

"John Weaver, if you don't stop your teasing, you'll have Fat Agnes's bread about your ears!"

She smiled one of her rare, toothless smiles.

"Aye, Goody'll be with you for Easter." She patted John's arm as he rose to take his leave. "Aye, and every Easter until young Harry weds. I've sworn by all that's holy that I'll not give up the ghost until I've laid Harry's first-born in his arms!"

John turned as he reached the gate.

"God keep you, Goody," he whispered, huskily.

"And you too, John Weaver. And mind you send that young blade to see old Goody when he comes home from school!"

Saints in Heaven, thought the old midwife as she hobbled back to her fire, it seems but yesterday that I brought Meg's babe into the world and christened him Harry. It seems but yesterday. Would to God that it were.

"Ho there, Master Weaver! Well met, friend!"

"Diccon! Diccon, it is good to see you!"

Harry Weaver, heir to the title and manor of Aldbridge and Diccon, son of the village miller clasped hands and laughed with delight.

"You've come with my horse, Diccon?"

"Aye, I've come to take you home from school, Harry," he teased, and dodged a well-aimed blow to his ear. "My, but I've such tales to tell you. I scarce know where to begin."

"Is it good then, to go to sea?"

"Aye, 'tis good; and better still to sail with Sir Francis Drake."

"Francis Drake is a pirate!"

"Drake is a privateer, and that's mighty different. He does but take a little of the Spaniards' wealth, and they have plundered it from their American colonies. 'Tis only a little private dealing between Elizabeth Tudor and Spanish Philip. It works mighty well," he added, patting the pocket that hung from his belt.

"You are well-paid for your seafaring, Diccon?"

"Nay, we get little *pay*. We get our fair share of the bounty, though, and that's a deal better to own."

"You all share in the plunder?"

"That we do, Harry, from the Queen of England, down."

"The Queen? Surely she does not profit from such enterprises?"

"That she does. Elizabeth Tudor takes the largest slice, and Admiral Drake has a fair purse, too. Then the gentlemen of the crew get their cut and the seamen and the gunners and the pikemen—even Diccon, the cabin-boy! I've a fair fistful of gold to show for my pains, and I've a mind to make another trip with Sir Francis before I settle down. Next time I'll sail as a seaman, and that should set me up in life nicely."

"You plan to settle in Aldbridge again? Have you found a maid to wed?"

"Aye, Harry, and my mother and father have given me their blessing, if only," he grinned, "to keep me away from the smell of the sea."

Harry Weaver looked at the lean, weather-tanned body of his lifelong friend.

"You are grown tall, Diccon. You are almost as tall as me now, yet you are two years younger."

"Aye, Harry. 'Tis the sea. It makes boys into men."

"And I will be seventeen at Michaelmas, and still a schoolboy," pouted Harry.

"That's the way of the world, friend," grinned Diccon.

"*You* get your learning from books. I'm getting mine from Life. It's the same thing, in the end."

The Minster clock chimed out noon-day.

"What time do my parents expect me home?"

"They didn't say."

"Then if we stable and water the horses, there would be time for . . ."

"For a little mischief, Harry?"

Harry Weaver grinned sheepishly.

"Well, not *mischief*, exactly."

"Then 'tis a wench. I know from the soft look on your face. Is she a tavern wench?"

"No, she's not one of those."

"Have you had a wench yet, Harry?"

"No. No, I haven't. But most of the lads at school have," he added hastily. "Have *you* had a wench, Diccon?"

"That I have. All sailors have wenches. I took one at Tilbury before we sailed."

There was a small silence and Harry Weaver dropped his eyes and scuffed the earth with the toe of his boot.

"I could have a wench, Diccon, but I don't want one, now."

"How come?"

"There's a maid. She's so fair it makes my guts turn over to look at her."

"I see. And she's spoiled you for other maids?"

"Aye, that's about it, Diccon."

"And who is she, this wondrous creature?"

"There's the rub. I don't know Diccon. I don't know exactly where she lives. Somewhere by the Minster yard,

I fancy."

"Have you spoken to her, then?"

"No, I've not even spoken to her," Harry Weaver looked up miserably. "Once when we chanced to meet I could have, but my tongue got tied into a knot. What am I to do, Diccon? I want to wed her."

"What does Sir John say about it?"

"Hell's teeth, Diccon, I've not told my parents. What would you have me say? *'Sir, there is a maid in York city, I do not know her name or her parentage or where she lives, but I want her for my wife.'* He'd call me a calf-head, wouldn't he?"

"Then you'd best get yourselves better acquainted, and quick, for if she's so fair she'll be snapped from under your nose. And serve you right, too!"

"I know it. I lay awake at nights and think about it. How would *you* go about it, Diccon? You know more of the world than I do. You've sailed the seas and bedded a wench."

"I've learned a little of the ways of the seas, but when it comes to courting—well, I'm not all that good." He threw back his head and laughed. "Lord, Harry, I made a right mess of it that night in Tilbury. That doxy got her money easy, I'll tell you! I've a mind to try it again, though. Maybe I'd do better with a York doxy."

"Then you'll not come with me?"

"That I'll not, Harry Weaver. I want a wench, I tell you. Go and do your courting on your own!"

"Then I'll see you here, at the school, at about three on the clock? Will that suit you?"

"Aye, three hours should just about give me time,"

bragged Diccon with an impish grin. "I'll see to the horses. Be off, and seek out your maid!"

"Three o'clock, then. Good hunting, Diccon!"

"Three o'clock. Good gawping, Harry!"

With a scuffle of fists, the friends parted.

It was almost two when Harry Weaver looked over the rooftops to the Minster clock.

I'll give it another minute, he thought. I'll give it till two on the clock, then I'll wait here no longer.

But where else to look for his love? He had seen her several times before leaving the Minster yard and making towards the King's Manor. Where else might she be in this teeming city? He had waited by the alley that led into the yard for nearly two hours. Surely he had not missed her?

His heart gave a giddy skid and he swallowed hard to quiet the pulse that pounded suddenly in his throat. Was she ill? There had been the sweating sickness in the city for several weeks.

"Mother of God," he prayed silently, "let her not be stricken."

Then, as though invisible hands had laid themselves on his shoulders and turned him around, he saw her walking slowly towards him. And all the pulses in his body began to throb and the dull thudding of his heart echoed in his ears. He ran his tongue round his lips. This time he would speak to her.

Their bodies almost touched as she side-stepped into the narrow alley.

"Mistress?" Harry pleaded.

The girl stopped for an instant and lifted her downcast eyes and the flicker of a smile played about her lips. Then she looked away from him and hurried past.

How long he stood there, spellbound, he did not know.

"Damn you for a fool, Harry Weaver," he said out loud and jerked himself into action.

As he reached the bottom of the alley he caught a glimpse of white-gold hair and feet that scarcely touched the ground as she ran over the cobblestones. Then a door thudded behind her and she was gone.

"God in Heaven, what ails me?"

They had been close, so close he could have held out his hand and touched her, yet he had acted like a lovesick sheep. She had looked into his eyes and she had smiled at him. A little smile, perhaps, but *she had smiled*. And her eyes. They were the blue of periwinkles. Were there, in the whole of the wide world, eyes as big and blue as hers?

The periwinkle eyes faded and Harry became aware of another pair of eyes, brown eyes, that gazed up from where an urchin sat in the gutter.

"Young master?"

"Aye?"

The brown eyes did not waver.

"Well?" snapped Harry.

With a slight turn of his head the urchin indicated the door that only seconds before had slammed shut.

"You know her, boy? You know that maid?"

"I might."

Harry reached in his purse for a groat, but the brown eyes stayed steadfast. Another groat.

"Who is she? Tell me who she is and I will give you two groats."

"She is Mistress Woodhall."

"Yes?"

A silver coin was held tantalisingly in the air.

"Listen, boy. If you will answer my questions and answer them with truth, I will give you a silver piece."

"Her name is Elizabeth Woodhall, though most people call her Beth."

Elizabeth Woodhall. Beth. Her very name made music.

"And is she pledged?"

The boy gave a derisive spit.

"Nay she is not pledged. Her father is a tyrant. None go courting at that house!"

"Her father? What does he do?"

"He works at the King's Manor. I think he is a clerk."

Beth. Her name was Beth and she was not pledged. Joyfully Harry flipped the silver coin then added the two groats for good measure.

Beth, *his* Beth, was not pledged. God bless her tyrant of a father!

"Did you do well, Diccon?"

"I did well, Harry! And you?"

Harry Weaver grinned. "Her name is Beth."

"Heaven be praised. So you untied your tongue at last?"

"Well, yes and no. But she is not pledged and her father, they say, is a tyrant, so none dare court her."

"And . . . ?"

34

"She is a modest maid, Diccon, but she smiled at me. She stopped for an instant and she smiled."

"Then I would say, Master Weaver," Diccon answered with mock severity, "that you are as good as at the church door!"

"Be serious, Diccon, and listen to me. Her father is a clerk, and works at the King's Manor. Tyrant or not, he must surely see what I have to offer Beth?"

"You would offer for her? You are truly serious about the maid? Her father is a clerk. You, Harry, are the son of a nobleman. You could not wed her."

"These are modern times, Diccon. Often people wed out of their station nowadays. Why, noblewomen have wed their horse-keepers before now and got away with it."

"Aye, when they were too old for anything better, I don't doubt."

"Does it matter? Things are changing. I will speak to my father when his mood is right. After all, I am not a bad match for any maid, am I Diccon?"

"No you are not. You will one day be a man of title and your wife a lady. You are a good match for any maid, let alone the daughter of a clerk."

"I care not what her parents are. I want her, Diccon and I'll marry her, I tell you!"

Diccon did not reply, for suddenly there was nothing to say.

Mistress Elizabeth Woodhall. Beth. Beth Weaver. The Lady Elizabeth Weaver.

Harry's thoughts ran riot. God, but was she not wondrous fair? Her hair was the pale gold of spring sunlight —and her eyes! He could imagine her eyes looking into his and her soft hair spread over the pillow beneath her head. And his arms would be round her in that great bed of his.

She would be easy to love, his Beth. He would give her many children. Red-headed lads and sweet little maids with white-gold hair. He would work for her and defend her always. He would love her for ever.

When he and Beth were old—like his own parents— they would still be in love. His own parents had made a love-match, had they not? They would understand. And then the blue eyes swam before his and he cared nothing if his parents understood or not.

There was a throbbing in his loins that set his whole body on fire. He wanted Beth Woodhall in his arms, in his bed, with the child of their love safe beneath her heart.

"You are silent, Harry. We have ridden these ten miles without a word. What are you thinking about?"

Jerked from his bed of white-hot passion, Harry Weaver begged Diccon's question.

"You too are silent, Diccon. What are you thinking about?"

"I was thinking of wenches and wenching."

"And I too was thinking about the same thing. A little in the future, maybe, but much the same thing, Diccon."

They dug their heels into their horses' flanks for they could see Weaver's Oak and the crossroads and home was but a spit away.

CHAPTER THREE

"My Lady Mother, I am home!"

With a yell of delight Harry Weaver jumped from his horse and clattered up the steps of the manor house.

"Come, Diccon. Leave the horses to the boy," he called. "Saints, I am so hungry my belly is touching the bones in my back!"

"Mother!"

Anne Weaver was swept off her feet as Harry's eager young arms enfolded her.

"Put me down, you wicked youth!" she laughed amid a flurry of petticoats and a hug that almost crushed her ribs. "John! John love, the lad is home!"

She held her son at arm's length and looked into his face. There was a sprinkling of fine fair down on his cheeks and upper lip, and his voice was now that of a man.

"Your hair is untidy and in need of a barber," she pronounced severely as she smoothed the unruly red-gold curls.

"Leave off, my lady," grinned Harry. "Diccon is watching, and I'll warrant his mother doesn't fondle *his* hair."

Diccon grinned.

"That she does, Harry, for all I am a man and go to sea!"

Anne held out her hands. Once, not so very long ago, she could have placed her arms round the shoulders of both Harry and Diccon. Now they had outgrown her and towered above her, and she was both glad and sorry.

"Come, boys, your supper is laid in the small parlour."

"What have you prepared, Mother, for the weary travellers?"

"There is wheat-bread and cheese and butter. And apples baked in honey to follow."

"No meat for a grown man?"

"*No meat,*" affirmed Anne, "until the fast is over on Sunday."

"The Lenten feast is old-fashioned, mother. Many people do not keep it now. Lack of good red meat saps a man's strength. Why must *we* keep the Lenten fast?"

"Because your lady mother says we must!"

John Weaver was standing in the doorway, a slow smile of pleasure spreading over his face at the sight of the boisterous youth. Then, like Anne, he held his son at arm's length.

"My, but you are grown tall, lad, since Christmas. What do they give you for victuals at St. William's? Beanpoles?"

"I am too tall for a schoolboy, father. Can I not be done with my schooling, and settle down in Aldbridge? I must learn the ways of the manor and the farming. Greek and Latin and figuring are a waste of a man's time when he is close on seventeen!"

"Settle down? Ho, young master! You are talking of settling down, are you? You'll be telling us next you are thinking of taking a wife!" John laughed uproariously.

"Come now, youngling, and eat your supper. You can leave your schooling after your birthday in September, and not one day before."

For a brief moment the joy of his homecoming was dulled and Harry was silent. What was so strange in a man wanting to take a wife? Then he was all smiles again.

"At Michaelmas, sir? Your word I can leave school at Michaelmas?"

"My word."

The time was not right, thought Harry Weaver, to mention Beth Woodall. Not tonight, when his belly ached with hunger and Diccon was seated at their supper table. Tomorrow maybe, when the excitement of his homecoming had abated. But mention Beth he would! And when they had met her they would love her as he loved her, of that, in his eager young heart, he was sure.

"And now," Anne passed the bread board and the dish of butter, "we will have all your news."

"First, madam," Harry broke a piece of cheese and stuffed it into his mouth, "I thank you for your letter."

Anne smiled proudly.

"You read it well?" she asked.

It had taken the best part of a morning to write that letter, she recalled. Learning did not come easily when a woman was past her middle-age. When, with sudden swiftness she had become the wife of a man of title, it had been necessary that she should learn to read and write and figure. It had been a laborious business, but

39

with her usual stubbornness she had overcome the shortcomings of her youth.

"I read it well, my lady," Harry smiled. "You have a fine fair hand."

"What of my coat of arms, sir?" Harry turned to his father. "It is not right that the arms of Sir Crispin Wakeman should rest over the door of our house, still. When will you pull them down and put our badge in their place?"

"Pull them down, lad? Nay, they are chiselled into the stonework. It would be a mighty expensive venture to do that. Sir Crispin's arms must remain. After all, he once lived here. His arms are part of the manor house."

He set down his knife and walked over to the cupboard, drawing from it a rolled parchment.

"See now, how does this suit you, young sir?"

Carefully he smoothed the drawing on the table.

"Here are the arms of the Weavers, lad. See, there is the rose for York and for Elizabeth Tudor; and the wheatsheaf and weaver's shuttle, so you may not in pride forget that once you came from the humble stock of one who was a weaver and farmer."

"And the flower?" Harry pointed to the little pansy that wound itself round the stem of the rose. "For what does the pansy stand?"

"It is a heartsease, Harry. A wild pansy. It was your sister's flower. We placed it there for Meg."

"My sister's flower? Is that why you'll not have them pulled up, father, even though they grow wild like weeds? Is that why the villagers will not tread on a heartsease? I thought it was but a local custom."

"Maybe it has become a local custom," John Weaver was instantly serious, "but it is true. None step on a heartsease, or uproot a plant. I asked it of them many years ago, and they understand, and respect Meg's memory."

"What was she like, sir? Harry's sister?" Diccon spoke for the first time.

Anne's eyes softened and she gazed into the fire as if she were trying to conjure a picture from the flames.

"She was slight and fair and beautiful. Her hair was pale, pale yellow. Her eyes were blue and she loved the tiny heartsease flowers. She embroidered them round the neck of her first grown-up dress."

Aye, whispered her thoughts, the dress we laid her in when she died. The dress she wore the night that Kit Wakeman had his way. The night they got *you*, Harry, their love-child.

"Tell me again. How did she die, my sister?"

"She was falsely accused of witchcraft by one who bore her a grudge," Anne countered. "A mob stoned her and she was hit on her head. It addled her brain and she died —the night after you were born. The good God takes, and the good God gives."

Aye, sweet lad, she died after she had given you life. She died calling for Kit Wakeman, who left this world a traitor, the devil take his evil soul!

John Weaver's gentle heart could feel his wife's torment.

"This was to be a surprise for you, Harry," he said, too eagerly, too quickly. "These drawings were sent from the wood carver in Ripon. He is to make our crest from fine Yorkshire oak, and your mother wishes it to be placed over the fireplace in the great hall. Perhaps it will be done in time for the Michaelmas Feast. How does that suit you?"

"It suits me fine, father," Harry grinned, "and my sons will be proud of it."

"Your sons, young blade?" laughed John. "I'd advise you first to find a wife to mother them!"

Diccon's eyes met Harry's.

"Aye, sir, I'll warrant you that." Painstakingly he spooned sweet honey sauce on his apples. "I shall not put the cart before the horse."

Diccon remained silent, and for that Harry was grateful.

"What of York? I have not seen the market since before Christmas time." Anne handed her husband a horn of ale. "We must journey to York soon, John."

"York is a place of unrest at this time, my lady." John's eyes were troubled. "There has been the sweating sickness in the back streets, and there is the matter of Mistress Clitheroe. Later we will go to York when the sickness has abated. Thank God Harry has not been tainted with it."

"Have you not heard, father? Mistress Clitheroe is dead."

"Dead?" Anne's spoon clattered to her plate. "They have killed her?"

"Aye, two days gone."

"But why? What has she done?"

"They said she harboured Catholic priests from Douai."

"And they hanged her for *that?*"

"They did not hang her, madam. She was crushed."

"Crushed? A woman!"

"Aye. And they said at school she was with child."

"God in Heaven, what of her bairns?"

Tears sprang to Anne Weaver's eyes.

"I know not, madam."

John Weaver shook his head sadly.

"Poor foolish woman. I'd leave have a live mother than a dead martyr. God rest her brave soul."

"God rest her," Anne whispered. "How was she Harry?"

"They said she was brave, mother, and prayed for the queen. We were not allowed from the school that morning. They took her from the prison on the bridge to the Toll Booth. There were many who watched, and she would have walked naked but they let her wear her shroud. She sewed it herself. The kitchen maid at the school said the sergeants who were to do it baulked and paid four beggars to take their place."

"Aye, it follows. Some men would do for their own mothers for a crust. Was it bad for her?"

"They laid a jagged stone beneath her back, then laid a heavy oak door on her and great stone slabs—"

"Stop!"

"It was very quick, they said, mother. It took but a few minutes."

Anne Weaver stood up, the legs of her chair grating harshly on the floor.

"I have amind to be alone," she said and hurried from the room.

Instantly Harry was on his feet.

"Nay lad, leave her," said John Weaver. "She's doubtless away to the church. Leave her be with her grief."

"I'm sorry, father. I would not have mentioned it had I known."

"Your mother would have heard sooner or later. Don't fret yourself."

But John knew the torment of Anne's mind. It seemed so wrong when there was but one God and one Heaven that it mattered in what fashion men prayed. But the Douai priests were slipping into the country and were sworn to kill Elizabeth Tudor. Had not the Pope declared it was no sin for a Catholic to kill the Queen? Why did Rome meddle?

Now Anne would be weeping on her knees for poor Mistress Clitheroe and doubtless too, for Meg. Meg had died all those years ago because she had learned of the plotting of Northern Catholics to rise up against Elizabeth Tudor. Hadn't Kit Wakeman accused her of witchcraft before a mob of hungry beggars to still her tongue and protect his fellow conspirators? Was it all to start again?

"Harry, lad. I think I'll seek out your mother. She is in great distress and needs comfort. Finish your victuals."

But Harry Weaver had lost his appetite.

That night the Lady Anne lay wide-eyed, tracing in the moonlight the intricate moulding of her bedchamber ceiling, mourning for three motherless bairns and an unborn child, and remembering her own sweet Meg of the heartsease.

And Harry tossed amid the unaccustomed softness of his feather bed and thought too about Meg and the fairness of her hair and the blueness of her eyes. Soft fair hair and blue eyes and Beth, *his* Beth.

Tomorrow he would tell Goody Trewitt when he visited her, about Beth. Goody would help him.

"Lord, how my knees ache!"

Goody Trewitt hobbled to her chair by the fire.

"Well, that's Good Friday's penance over, thanks be to God. Throw some logs on the fire, Harry lad. Yon church is as cold as charity!"

"Goody Trewitt, you are bossy as ever!"

"Aye lad, and you suddenly, are a man."

She shook her head, muttering half to herself and half to the back of the youngling bent at the hearth with the bellows in his hand.

"It seems but yesterday it all happened."

"What happened, Goody?"

"The night you were born, Harry. The night I laid you in my arms and christened you for the old king."

"Why did *you* christen me, Goody? Why was I not carried to the church?"

"You were, lad, later. But old Father Sedgwick, God rest him, was a priest who sat astride the fence. The uprising was brewing, and he didn't know on which side to get off."

"But why should he not baptise me? What had the uprising to do with a new-born babe?"

Goody shifted uneasily and picked up the stocking she was knitting.

"Father Sedgwick wanted an easy living. He was a Catholic priest who turned his coat when Harry Tudor was at loggerheads with Rome. Sedgwick took a wife and conformed to the Anglican church. But he'd as leave have cast her off and got out his bell and incense again if the uprising had put Mary Stuart on Elizabeth's throne. He'd have taken up with the old religion at the drop of a hat."

"But why would he not baptise me when I was born?"

"Like I said, he was a frightened man. Your sister had been accused of witchcraft. He would have nothing to do with the family," Goody prevaricated.

Harry sat back on his heels and looked closely at the old woman.

"My mother was old when she had me, wasn't she, Goody?"

"Old for child-bearing, yes. She had no milk for you."

"Aye, my mother told me that. 'Goody Trewitt,' she said, 'conjured up a wet nurse.' "

"Simple Polly? She wasn't right in the head, wasn't Polly, but her milk was good. Her babies were always stillborn which was an act of God, if you ask me, and there was always some woman glad of Polly's milk. She made a good living on it for many years and all the babies she suckled have grown up strong and strapping, like yourself."

"My sister was much older than me, wasn't she, Goody?"

"Aye. By close on seventeen years."

"And she was very beautiful?"

"She was fair as an April morning. There was an air about her, as though she were already half gone from this world. She was a dreamer, Harry."

"Was she pledged?"

"She was pledged to Diccon's father. She would have married him on her eighteenth birthday."

"And her flower was the heartsease?"

Goody set down her needles. Harry Weaver, suddenly, was being a mite too curious.

"Why all these questions, lad? You've never bothered your head about the past before. You are growing up. Look to the future, and let your sister rest in peace."

Harry Weaver remained silent, staring into the flames in the hearth.

"Your father was a hard-working yeoman and your mother was once a kitchen-maid at the manor," Goody urged, "at that very house which one day will be your own. It suited Elizabeth Tudor to give that manor of Sir Crispin Wakeman's to your father, and thence to you. Count your blessings, lad, and thank God for your good parents. Let the past lie, Harry!"

"I do not worry about the past, Goody. I know my sister was falsely accused. But I am growing up. I'm to leave school at my seventeenth birthday, and—"

He stopped, his cheeks flushing red.

"And there's a wench?"

"Aye, there's a wench."

"Tell Goody about her."

The old woman was glad to be away from the past. Harry Weaver, for all the world knew, was the son of

Sir John and the Lady Anne. Only Elizabeth Tudor and Jeffrey Miller and herself knew otherwise. Goody Trewitt wanted to forget the part she had played in the deception.

"Well, that was why, I suppose, I wanted to know about Meg."

"What has Meg to do with it?"

"Beth—that's her name—seems to be powerful like Meg was. Beth is so beautiful that my heart jerks at the sight of her. Beth's hair is long and pale and her eyes are blue, like Meg's were."

"And what have your parents said in the matter?"

"They do not know. I haven't told them yet."

"*Told* them? Don't you think it would be a mite better if you were to *ask* them?"

"You know what I mean, Goody. And anyway, it would seem a bit stupid if I told them the plain truth of it. I haven't spoken yet to Beth. I follow her about like a love-sick sheep, and wait hours for the sight of her. I was flogged at school not long since for playing truant to catch sight of her."

"It's not just calf love, think you, Harry?"

"It's not calf love. I want her for my wife."

"Maybe she is pledged."

"No, she is not. I know that for certain."

"Then what is her station in life? You are the son of a nobleman, Harry. You must make a fitting marriage."

"Her father is a clerk. He works sometimes at the King's Manor and sometimes at the Treasurer's house in York."

"Then it would not be seemly, would it, for you to

take the maid out of her station? She cannot marry above herself."

"Goody, this is 1586! These are modern times. My mother and father were lifted above their station, were they not?"

"That they were, because the Queen decreed it. But there are things that are done and things that are not done. Marrying out of class is still one of them, despite the times."

"Then I'll throw away my inheritance. I can marry her then!"

"Foolish boy. A while ago I thought you were growing up!"

Harry Weaver stared ahead, his mouth set tight in defiance. He was like Anne Weaver, Goody thought. Stubborn and unyielding when he thought himself to be in the right. And there was a streak in him, too, of Kit Wakeman. Kit Wakeman had been determined to have Meg. It was natural that Harry should have inherited some of the wilful blood of his father. At least, she conceded, Harry wanted his maid in wedlock, which was more than could be said for his natural father.

"I want Beth Woodhall."

Harry spoke the words slowly and forcefully and Goody knew her taunt had had no effect.

"Then what would you have Goody do?"

"Help me?"

"How can I help you, Harry? 'Tis none of my business, and well you know it."

"At least then, try to see my reasoning. Don't condemn me out of hand."

49

"Nay lad, I'll not do that."

Goody understood more than Harry knew. Anne and John Weaver had made a love-match. Theirs had been no prearranged contract to unite great families and merge large estates. They had been happy though they had known sorrow and hardship. They were still happy. Surely then young Harry had some right to choose his own mate as they had done?

"Don't rush into things, Harry. You don't know for certain that the maid will have you. She'll need to be courted a bit first. Give it a little while and see how things turn out. It may be that a way out of the wood can be found."

Please God, let it be so, she prayed. There had been none other than Kit Wakeman for Meg, even though she had known they could never wed. Even though they were both pledged to another. Now it was happening again, and who, this time, would be hurt?

"You think so, Goody?"

Now the despondent boy was happy again.

"You *will* help me?"

"Leave it, Harry. There's naught to be lost by going easy. Your own parents' marriage is a happy one, and they were love-matched. Maybe I can put in a word here and there that will help. But hold your horses, young gallant. Take it easy."

"And you don't condemn me, Goody?"

"No lad, I don't condemn you. I'd like fine to see you happily wed. I'm an old woman, Harry. So old that I have lost the tally. But I've vowed by God's good grace that I'll stay alive until I've placed your first-born into your arms. I brought Meg into the world and it was Goody's hand that slapped the life into you. And I'll not go until I hear the lusty bawling of your son. But easy does it, Harry, and remember what I tell you."

Goody reached to where the youngling sat at her feet and stroked his mop of curls. God, she thought, but he fathered himself. Had others in the village remembered Kit Wakeman's red-gold hair? It was well if they had, that none seemed to have mentioned it.

"I'll remember, Goody. You will say nothing to my parents just yet?"

"I will say nothing."

"Then I will take my leave. You'll be with us at the manor on Sunday, for the Easter Feast?"

"I'll be there. I'll swear to you Harry that my one besetting sin is my belly. I'd not miss one of your mother's feasts!"

"Then Mistress Goody, it will be my pleasure to call for you and give you my arm."

Goody Trewitt smiled.

"You are an imp, Harry Weaver, but you are a good boy and I will pray with all my heart for your happiness."

At the doorway Harry Weaver paused.

"And you, Goody Trewitt are my dearest and my most trusted friend—next to Diccon—and I love you!" he grinned.

"Aye, Harry, and I love you too," the old nurse whispered to the empty room. "I love you as I loved your sweet pretty mother before you. I'd have given my eyes to have seen her happy."

She gazed into the dancing flames of the fire as it trying to recall a ghost from the past.

"Meg, my pretty," she whispered, "you gave a fine son to the world. A fine son."

CHAPTER FOUR

THE horses fretted to be off, their hooves scraping the cobbles of the stable-yard, their backs already slung with Harry's packs.

"Where *are* Diccon and Jeffrey?"

Harry Weaver too, was eager to be gone, for the Easter holidays were over and he had not seen Beth for almost a month.

"Why can I not go to York to pay the tithe money?" he had asked his father, glad of any excuse to ride into the city.

But John had refused his request.

"Jeffrey always carries the tithe money to the Council. It will wait until you return to your school. Diccon can ride with you both, and that will be an extra safeguard against footpads."

"What keeps Jeffrey?" fumed Harry to his parents. "The sun has been up this hour and still he has not come."

"Jeffrey will come," replied John Weaver. "And what makes you so eager, young master, to be back to your schooling? I'll warrant 'tis the first time you ever showed any inclination to be back at your desk."

Harry Weaver ran his fingers through his riot of red-gold curls and looked at the toes of his boots.

"It's my last term, sir. I am eager to make a start and be done with it," he lied.

He must be more careful. He had nearly given the game away. Did his eagerness to see Beth show so plainly? He had tried, more than once, to tell his parents about her, yet the time had not seemed right.

But Goody Trewitt knew about Beth and had promised her help. It seemed so stupid that a man must marry one of his own station in life. Why should love-matches be only for the working-class?

"You have your box of sweetmeats, and your money for ink and paper?"

"Aye, mother. And my goose-quills are sharpened and packed.'

"And you will not forget your parents each night in your prayers?"

"That I will not, madam."

"And you will pray for the Queen, also? Lord knows Her Grace needs our prayers."

"I will pray for the Queen, mother."

Anne Weaver patted the strong young hand. Harry was quite right. He was almost a man, now. It was fitting he should be done with schooling. Her heart turned over with pride as she looked at the tall, straight youngling, stuffing his wilful curls beneath his cap. How proud Meg would have been of her son.

She must speak to John, Anne decided, about a wife for Harry. Already she had three such maids in her mind's eye. Modest little wenches, all of them, with a good family behind them and robust with health. Harry must have sons to follow him.

A shout of laughter broke into her thoughts and Jeffrey and Diccon walked through the yard-gate.

"Bid you a fine morning, Sir John! My lady!"

Respectfully, Jeffrey Miller tipped his cap. Already Harry was unhitching his horse's reins.

"You are late, Jeffrey. What kept you?"

"Such news!" The miller's face creased into a grin. "We have a daughter! My Judith was safely delivered about four of the clock, this morning!"

Anne Weaver held out her arms to Jeffrey.

"A little maid, at last, on St. Mark's Day. I am so glad for you both, Jeffrey. Is Judith well?"

"Aye, my lady. She had no trouble. Mistress Trewitt was with her. And my mother."

"But can you be spared, Jeffrey?" John Weaver asked, anxiously.

"Spared, Sir John? That I can! The house is full of women, coo-ing and clucking over the little babe. They're glad to get me and Diccon from under their feet."

"Have you named her yet?"

"That I have, my lady. Judith picked the names for our sons. 'Give me a daughter, Jeffrey Miller,' she always said, 'and *you* shall name her.' So this morning, I looked at my little maid, and there was only one name I could give her. Her hair is fair and fine as thistle-seed, and her eyes are big, and blue like cornflowers. She is to be Margaret."

"Margaret?" Anne's eyes clouded with tears. "That was the name we gave to our little maid."

"Aye, my lady. I named her for Meg."

Anne Weaver gulped back the lump that rose in her throat. Here stood the man, now happily married, to whom they had given Meg's pledge. And, after almost twenty years, he had named his first-born daughter for her.

"Has she been christened yet?"

"No, madam. We plan to take her to church tomorrow."

"Then I would ask a favour for you and your wife, Jeffrey. Let me stand for the little one?"

"*You*, my lady?"

"Aye, Jeffrey. For the sake of times gone by?"

"You do us an honour. My Judith will be mortal proud."

"Then tomorrow, and you permit it, I will carry my god-daughter to her christening. I will stand for your little Meg, Jeffrey, and be very proud."

"Jeffrey! Let's be gone!"

Already Harry and Diccon were astride their horses. John Weaver grinned at the impatience of youth.

"He seems mortal eager to be back to his books, the young varmint!"

"Or his little wench," laughed Jeffrey.

"His *wench*?"

John Weaver crossed his forehead into a puzzled frown, and Jeffrey knew he had said the wrong thing.

"Nay, Sir John. It was but boyish teasing I overheard between Diccon and Harry. 'Tis the way boys talk when they think they are men!"

"Aye, doubtless you are right, Jeffrey. The tithe money is in the pouch of the saddle-bag of your mare."

John cupped his hand to help Jeffrey mount. "You know what to do with it?"

"Aye, Sir John. *And* wait on a written receipt from the clerk."

"Then God go with you all."

One by one the horses passed beneath the stable-yard archway, their hooves clattering on the cobblestones.

Harry raised his hand in salute to his parents, then grinned happily to Molly and Fat Agnes as they waved from the kitchen window.

This was the last time he would ride out of the manor house as a schoolboy. When he came back he would be done with it all, and a man. And when he returned, he swore, he would have Beth's pledge safe, and it would be a love-pledge.

He cared nothing for her tyrant of a father. He could offer Beth the Manor of Aldbridge and a fine home and servants. He could give his protection for all time, and the wealth and title that one day would be his. And most of all, he could give her his love.

Wheeling their horses to the left-hand as they reached the crossroads at the brow of the hill, Harry jabbed his horses's flanks with the heels of his boots, setting it into a canter.

"Come, Diccon," he yelled joyfully. "The last man to Micklegate Bar buys the ale!"

Before them lay the fine straight road and at either side of them fields lush and green with young wheat and barley. And beyond the fields lay the common-land, skirting the thick forest of oak and beech where robbers and footpads lurked, and outlaws found refuge.

But on this fine April morning, the long ride to York with the tithe money and the prospect of months of school books and inky fingers did not deter Harry Weaver. Beyond the forest, but fifteen miles away, lay the walls of York and Beth Woodhall.

"Lord save us, Harry. Is the devil at your heels?" shouted Diccon as he urged his horse forward.

But Harry Weaver did not reply. He threw back his head to the soft spring day and laughed out loud.

For a long time after the horses were gone from sight and the beat of their hooves lost from sound, John Weaver stood by the stable-yard gateway. He had sensed that Harry's explanation of his eagerness to be back to York was not all that it should be. Boyish boasting it may be, but John knew there was more than a mite of truth in Jeffrey's hastily explained excuse.

Perhaps, in a week or two, he would himself ride into York. Anne had expressed a wish, had she not, to visit the market there? He could leave Anne at her cousin's house, maybe, and be free to get to the bottom of the mystery, in his own way.

And a mystery it was, for it was unlike Harry to be underhanded. They had reared him to respect the truth. A casual boyish fancy would surely have been mentioned, but Harry had said nothing. And Harry had within him a streak of Kit Wakeman's wilfulness and not a little of Meg's stubbornness. It was natural that it should be so. But one thing was certain. This matter must be nipped in the bud before it flourished and bloomed.

Many years ago, they had been faced with another such problem when Meg had prevaricated and begged some time before she and Jeffrey were married. And foolishly he had indulged that whim, overriding Anne's insistence that Meg would be better married and away from Kit Wakeman's reach. Anne had been right and he should have known it.

Was it to happen all over again? *Was* there anything in Jeffrey's chance remark? There was but one thing to do, and that was to get at the truth of the matter. Tonight, at suppertime John would tell Anne to start writing her shopping lists for the trip to York. It could do no harm, could it, to make sure?

"You look tired, friend," John Weaver handed a horn of ale to Jeffrey, "and I blame myself. The ride to York and back was too much to ask, after your disturbed night."

"Nay, Sir John, my night was one of joy, and I have often ridden to York and back without taking harm, and well you know it!"

He looked thoughtfully into the fire.

" 'Twas what happened in York that perplexes me."

"Harry?"

"No, Harry is well, be sure of that, Sir John. I left Harry and Diccon at the tavern in Petergate and went first to the King's Manor to safely deposit the tithe money. There's a clerk there, a Master Sykes, who usually attends to my business."

"Aye, Jeffrey, I know him well. What of him?"

Jeffrey Miller took a pull at his ale, then shook his head, grinning ruefully as he did so.

"You may call me a simpleton, Sir John, and I'll deserve it, but this day I saw . . . "

He stopped and shrugged his shoulders, then lifted his eyes to meet John Weaver's.

" . . . this day, at the King's Manor, I saw Kit Wakeman!"

There was no sound in the room. John Weaver did not speak.

"Well, Sir John? Tell me I am a goon!"

"You are no goon, Jeffrey. But tell me your story."

"I paid the money to Master Sykes and he counted every last groat of it; then wrote me a receipt. He's a surly fellow, yon Sykes, and not given to talk, let alone idle talk."

"But what has Sykes to do with Kit Wakeman?"

"It was Master Sykes who set me thinking. I'd have not given the matter another thought, but for him. I saw this fellow, and for all I'd have sworn it was Kit Wakeman, still I'd have laughed at myself for my fancies. Make no mistake, Sir John, it *was* Kit Wakeman, or the devil himself! A man can change much in near on twenty years, But I'd recognise the arrogance of that wicked youngling and the bearing of him after a hundred years! And there was no mistaking his hair. He had it cropped short, but still it curled round his head, with hardly a trace of grey in the red of it. He was crossing the yard and on his way towards the Treasurer's House, and my stomach churned fit to make me sick at the sight of him. I do not know if he recognised me, or even saw me. After all, I am more changed than he, and he would not know me, I doubt."

"And Master Sykes?"

"Well, Sir John, I was so bemused that I found myself walking back to Master Sykes' counting house. 'Tell me,' I asked him, 'yon fellow with the red hair. I seem to remember him from my youth.' And Master Sykes spoke loud and long against him. '*That* overbearing lick-spittle,' he said. 'He has the status of a clerk and the arrogance of a war-lord!' "

"Aye." John Weaver nodded his head. "It follows."

" 'I forget his name,' I said to Master Sykes, 'but I mind him well;' and Sykes told me his name was Cedric Woodhall, which confused me further."

"The name is different, Jeffrey, but not the letter. Don't you see? Kit—Christopher—Wakeman. Cedric Woodhall? The initials are alike. What else did Master Sykes have to say for himself?"

"He told me that Master Woodhall is an upstart. He said he rides to London, always with a Queen's Messenger, carrying despatches to Sir Francis Walsingham. And Master Sykes declared that was not the thing for a humble clerk to do."

"Then if it *was* Kit Wakeman you saw, he has turned his coat. Walsingham is a zealous Protestant and a hunter of Catholic priests. But I'll tell you something, Jeffrey. At the time, Lady Anne said I was sickening for an ague, and put me to bed with a sleeping posset, and in the morning I was determined to heed her words and put it from my mind. It happened four weeks gone, at the crossroads, by Meg's grave."

And John Weaver told his story, and when he had done, Jeffrey did not scold or disbelieve him as Anne had done.

"You saw no devil that night, Sir John. And mark my words, Kit Wakeman has not turned his coat. Master Sykes said Woodhall was known to frequent the Mass House in Coppergate."

"But that would tally, Jeffrey. If Wakeman—Woodhall—call him what you will, is somehow in Sir Francis Walsingham's pay, does it not follow that he would visit houses where Mass is said, if only to spy on Catholics and Catholic priests?"

"Aye, Sir John, mayhap you are right. But why should Kit Wakeman aid a Protestant? And one so near to the Queen, at that? With Spain and France declaring they will soon restore the old faith to England, would not Kit Wakeman do all in his power to help put a Catholic ruler on Elizabeth Tudor's throne? Once, remember, he rebelled against Elizabeth, in favour of Mary Stuart?"

"And lost his head for his treason, along with young Norton, or so I'd have sworn, many years ago. You mind the time I went to London at the Queen's command. I saw Kit Wakeman's head stuck on a pole on London Bridge. And there was a trooper with me—Martin, his name was—who said he remembered the younglings. One, he said, had been called Norton. The other he knew not. But *I* knew him, Jeffrey. For all the head was rotted, that red hair marked him. I'd have sworn on Harry's life it was Kit Wakeman's head I saw that day."

"And now you think you could have been wrong?"

"I *know* I was wrong. Kit Wakeman is alive, and a traitor to his country, still. He has much to gain if Mary Stuart or some other Catholic Prince were seated on England's throne. The Manor of Aldbridge, for one thing, and John Weaver for another, dangling on the gibbet-elm by Aldbridge crossroads!"

"Then why does he work for Sir Francis Walsingham if he visits mass houses?"

"He doesn't visit mass houses to spy. He visits them because he has a Catholic soul, and always will have. If he is working for Walsingham, he's playing a double game, and that I tell you. And who better fitted in his evil than Kit Wakeman to play such a game?"

"Then I will kill him, Sir John, and it will be my pleasure. Who would miss him, anyway? As far as the world knows, he died a traitor's death long since."

"No Jeffrey. You are a good man and I'll not have you taint your hands. Kit Wakeman is *my* pigeon to pluck. Leave it to me for a while, and I'll think what's to be done."

"But you'll let me aid you? I, too, have an old score to settle. For Meg's sake, I have that right."

"I shall do nothing without I tell you first," John promised. "But you must give me your word you'll say not one word to a living soul about what you saw in York or what I have told you this night."

"I'll swear it, Sir John, on Meg's grave and on my own little Meg's sweet life."

"Then go home to Judith and your little babe, Jeffrey. I shall pour myself a draught of barley wine and take myself into the parlour with my thoughts."

But John Weaver was allowed precious little time with his thoughts, for he had not reckoned with Goody Trewitt.

"Lord, John Weaver," she declared as she heaved her quivering bulk into the chair opposite, "I am all those things the devil devised to make an old woman miserable. I am hungry, I am thirsty and I am tired!"

John set down his goblet.

"Your hunger and thirst shall be taken care of, Goody, and a good night's rest will do much to relieve your labours of last evening."

"Last evening, John Weaver?"

"Aye, Goody. Jeffrey has told us about his new babe."

"Nay, that was nothing. Judith Miller was no trouble. She is a woman born to motherhood. I was with her but a couple of hours. 'Twas the other . . . " She stopped, abruptly. "I did not sleep well."

"*The other*, Goody? Where were you last evening?"

"I was nowhere, I tell you. I did not sleep, and that's the truth of it."

Goody Trewitt was relieved when Anne walked into the room.

"I am hungry, Anne Weaver. This afternoon I dozed in my chair and when I awoke the fire was dead and my cooking pot cold. You wouldn't have a chicken leg or two for an old midwife, would you?"

"No Goody, I would not. But there is cold beef and perhaps a slice of sugared plum-cake to follow. Will that suit you?"

"It will suit me nicely, Anne; and I thank you."

"Goody was up to mischief last night," John teased.

"So! You kept the graveyard vigil?"

"And what if I did?"

Trust Anne Weaver to put her finger straight on the truth!

"Goody," John admonished. "You know I have forbidden the graveyard vigil. It is heathen practice and well you know it. Who else kept watch with you?"

"I was there alone."

"The truth, Mistress Trewitt, on your sacred oath!"

"There was Barnabas the fox-catcher, and old Peter from the far croft. And we did harm to no one, John Weaver."

"Only to yourselves, Goody. I have spoken before about the graveyard watch. I thought you would have heeded my words."

"If I am to die, it's *my* business," snapped the old woman.

"If we are to die, Goody, it is God's Will," said Anne, gently. "We are none of us the better for knowing it."

"We harmed no one, I tell you."

"Goody, you are our dearest friend, and Anne and I worry about you. You'll do your old bones no good by waiting in a graveyard half the night. Tell me truly, have you ever seen a spirit on one of your vigils?"

"I have, John Weaver, I have."

"I do not believe you, Goody."

"John Weaver, if the good Lord in His wisdom chooses on St. Mark's Eve to make His Will known, who are you to gainsay Him?"

"It is superstition, Goody. No one will ever make me

believe that on the Eve of St. Mark, the spirits of those who are to die in the next twelve-month walk through the graveyard!"

"Then you may believe what you wish, and I will believe what I saw with my own eyes!"

"Saw? What did you see last night?"

"Only superstitious, heathen nonsense, Anne Weaver. It wouldn't interest *you*."

Anne's face was white now and her eyes dilated with fear. She had heard before of Goody's graveyard vigils and spirits or not, the old woman had foretold many deaths.

"Tell me, Goody," Anne almost pleaded.

"Lord, I do it every year and every year I say 'Never again.' I wish I had not done it yester-evening, and that's the truth of it. Oh, don't fret yourself, Anne. It was no one belonging to you. 'Twas no one in the village, truth known."

"Then who?"

"I don't rightly know, but just before one of the clock I saw her. She walked slowly and sadly, but she was proud. I could not see her face, but she passed by with a regal bearing. It was a queen, Anne. A queen is to die!"

"Mercy on us, the Queen!"

" 'Tis the Jesuits from Douai, that's what!" John Weaver had forgotten his scoffing. "They will kill the Queen! And what's to be done?"

"Naught is to be done," Goody replied sombrely, "for naught can be done. It is the will of God."

"Goody Trewitt, hear me and hear me good!" Now John Weaver's face had turned to anger. "I forbid you ever to keep the graveyard watch again. *Forbid,* I tell you. Next year I'll have the churchyard locked, and Father Sowerbye shall hear of this. He shall proclaim it from the pulpit on Sunday. There is to be no more of this!"

"Aye, John," whispered the old woman, miserably, "you are right. I'll tell you straight, I liked not what I saw last night."

And that very next Sunday, Father Sowerbye did justice to Sir John Weaver's wishes. Father Sowerbye's Hell fire and damnation would have gladdened the heart of the dour John Knox himself, so charged with fire and brimstone and eternal purgatory was it.

"And so I ask of you, good people—nay, I *demand* of you, that this heathen practice be stopped!" he ranted from the great height of his pulpit.

"Let those guilty ones take heed that the Church will not countenance this pagan folly."

He paused and looked round his flock, enjoying to the full, the fear and consternation on the faces upturned to his words.

"Take heed," he whispered.

The dropping of a feather would have been heard in that hushed congregation had it not been for the soft comfortable snoring of the one for whom the forceful warning had most been uttered. She had heard not one word of it for Goody Trewitt always slept through Father Sowerbye's sermons.

CHAPTER FIVE

A TIRED black bee grumbled overhead, searching for nectar in the weed-choked flower beds and high in the gaping ruins rooks and carrion crows squabbled like fishwives. The mid-July sun beat down on the old stones of the gutted church where not so long ago the Benedictine monks of St. Mary's Abbey had prayed.

"It is a mortal pity."

"A pity, sweeting?"

Harry Weaver lifted the cap that shaded his face and turned his head lazily on Beth Woodhall's lap.

"Aye. That a church should stand so ruined. My father says it is sacrilege."

"Nay, love. The Abbot of St. Mary's was getting too fat. He and his ilk deserved what they got. They were more powerful than the King."

"But to turn them out and ransack the Abbey seems to be setting God at defiance, don't you think?"

"Maybe, but those days are over. It happened when my father was a youngling, donkey's years ago. It doesn't concern us, little Beth."

"My father says it does, Harry. My father says there are many who will live to regret what Henry Tudor did to the Church."

Harry Weaver settled his cap afresh and closed his eyes again. It was comfortable dozing in the warm sun-

69

shine in the deserted gardens of the once beautiful abbey, his head resting on Beth's lap. To talk of the surly Master Woodhall was to spoil the beauty of the afternoon.

"Your father is away, Beth. Let's make the most of it, whilst he is gone."

He reached for the small soft hand that fondled his hair.

"It has been wonderful meeting you without fear of discovery. I wish he journeyed to London more often."

"Aye, and though it is wrong of me, I wish it, too. Why, my mother even smiles, sometimes, when he is gone from home."

"And my mother is just the opposite. She is lost and unhappy when my father is away, and worries about him the whole of the time."

Beth Woodhall twined a soft curl round her finger, sighing softly.

"And there lies the difference," she whispered sadly.

"The difference . . . ?"

"The difference between you and me, Harry."

Angrily the youth turned, pushing himself into a sitting position and taking the anxious face in his hands.

"We'll have no more of this talk, Mistress Beth. I love you, and though you'll not admit it, you love me, too."

Passionately he kissed the closed eyelids.

"We've gone over this many times before, and I'll not be gainsaid, I tell you. There is only one difference between us, and one that pleases me greatly!"

Vainly the unhappy girl tried to turn from the lips that soughts hers.

70

"No, Harry. Sometimes I think it can never be. You are noble-born, and I am . . . "

"You are my Beth. You are the woman I want!"

" . . . I am the daughter of a clerk."

"I don't care if Lucifer himself spawned you, so stop your protesting. Do you know what my father does when my mother scolds?"

Unspeaking, she shook her head.

"He kisses her, Beth. He kisses her till she is breathless and can scold no more. It is the only way to deal with it, my father says, and I've a mind to take a leaf from his copy-book!"

"It is strange and sweet to me that a man and his wife can be so. I have never seen my father and mother kiss."

"Not even when they have squabbled?"

"They do not squabble. I often wish they did. No, they speak when they must, but most times there is nothing. Just a silence, Harry. A silence so complete I can almost hear it screaming hatred."

"But they must have loved, once. They got you, didn't they?"

"Yes, and it seems mortal strange to me, for I cannot imagine it."

"You imagine over much, Beth. Why, who knows but what they are sweethearts when they are together in their bed?"

"My father sleeps in the garret room, Harry. *I* share my mother's bed. I tell you, they neither agree nor disagree. It is almost as if each of them lives in a world apart. If that is wedlock, I'd a mind to stay a spinster for the rest of my days."

"That you shall not. On my oath, that you shall not!"

"But I will never marry *you*, Harry. My mother wants me to promise to Giles, the coppersmith's apprentice, and my father will not hear of it. 'Wait,' he says. 'She will marry when I am good and ready and she'll marry into her rightful station in life.' And then my mother says that Giles is of our station, but my father just looks away from her and smiles mighty mysterious and says softly, 'There'll come a time . . . ' almost as if he were talking to himself. As if he knew something we did not."

"What does your father mean?"

"I don't know. I must wait, he says, until the time comes."

"He speaks in riddles, but for all that I am mighty grateful to him. After all, if your father thinks that a coppersmith is not good enough for you, maybe he would be pleased to give his daughter to the son of a nobleman. Had you thought of that, Beth?"

"And Sir John, your father? Would *he* be content for his son to marry beneath him?"

"Why not? Once my father was a weaver who also farmed a croft of land, and my mother was a kitchen-maid in Priory Street, not a spit from where we sit now. Then she went to Aldbridge to serve Sir Crispin Wakeman. My mother is now mistress of that house. Nothing is impossible, Beth. My father and mother were love-matched and they are happy, still. They will want a love-match for me, also."

"And when will you tell them?"

Harry lifted his eyes to where a small soft cloud lay white on a sky of summer blue.

"I tried to talk to my father when he was in York a month ago, but it was not possible. My mother was there and her cousin, and then my father had private business of his own and the time was lost. But I will talk to my parents about you, Beth. They have only wanted that I grow to happiness. They will love you, I know it."

He jumped to his feet, holding out his hands to her.

"See over yonder, the church that stands ruined. It must, once, have been a holy place. Come with me into the church, Beth, and give me your love-plight. The better the place, they say, the better the deed."

Fingers entwined they picked their way over mossy stones to where the empty doorway yawned. Above them the sky made a roof and the once majestic windows, long since gutted for their lead, gaped like holes in a sun-dried skull.

And at the end of the weed-grown aisle where sandalled feet once trod and monks prostrated themselves, Harry took Beth's hands in his.

"Here I think the altar stood. Give me your promise on this spot, Beth."

"What will I promise?"

"That you will love me always, sweeting. And if you love me always, there can never be another."

"I love you, Harry. I loved you that day, weeks back when first you spoke to me. You blushed like a schoolboy and all you said was 'Mistress?' I knew then I would love you for always."

"I *was* a schoolboy—I still am. But soon now I will be done with it and then we will be wed."

Gently he kissed her lips.

"I love you, Beth. I will love you into Eternity, and beyond. On this sacred spot I swear it."

Above them a thrush sang.

"Listen to the little mavis, Beth. He sings us a love song. Perhaps it is an answer from the Almighty."

On the crumbling altar he kissed her again and with a strange urgent passion that forbade denial.

It had been easier than he dared hope thought Sir John Weaver, to make yet another trip into York without arousing his wife's curiosity. He had been grateful to Jeffrey for giving him the opportunity.

"I must ride into York with this broken cog-wheel. Is there any service I can do for you or the Lady Anne while I am there?" he had asked

John had seized the chance and announced his intention to ride with Jeffrey. Anne did not question the trip, and merely requested that John visit St. William's and deliver a letter and a plum-cake to Harry.

"You had no luck on your last trip, Sir John?" asked Jeffrey as they settled down to a comfortable jog-trot.

"No, Jeffrey. I went as far as I could. without asking too many questions. That a Master Woodhall exists there is no doubt, but whether or not we can stop his little dance is another matter. This time, I must be more bold. It seems that Master Sykes at the King's Manor has no liking for Woodhall and might be bribed to give me the information I want. I think he is my best hope."

"And if you come across Woodhall and you agree with me that he is Kit Wakeman, what will you do, Sir John?"

74

"I think there is no doubt that Woodhall *is* Kit Wakeman. What I want to know is the game he is playing. That he is in Sir Francis Walsingham's pay is sure and his clerking is but a cover for it. I am almost as sure he is also working for the Jesuits and that is treason, in any true Englishman's language."

"And if you prove him to have a hand in treason, what then?"

"I don't know, Jeffrey. I could denounce him, but is it not best to let sleeping dogs lie? Kit Wakeman could harm Harry. The lad fondly believes that Lady Anne and myself are his parents. If Harry were to learn the truth of his birth, would he thank us for lying to him, all these years? It might come as a shock to know he was a bastard and his father a traitor. It would be like suddenly losing a mother and father and finding he had only grandparents who had lied to him."

"They were white lies, told to protect the innocent, Sir John."

"But lies, for all that. And the strange thing of it is, Jeffrey, that I have always felt myself to be his father."

But Jeffrey Miller had an old score to settle. Kit Wakeman had robbed him of his betrothed. It was for the youngling he had been that he sought revenge and not for the happily married man he now was. He had loved Meg with all his boyish heart, just as he now loved Judith with the strong sure love of a man. Kit Wakeman could not go unpunished, Jeffrey swore silently.

"Then there is but one thing to do, Sir John. Find proof of his treachery and then make our own justice. It is no crime to kill an enemy of the Queen."

"Would it not be better, Jeffrey, to hold his guilt over his head? Maybe we could demand that he left the country on pain of betrayal."

"And let a traitor go free? It is the bounden duty of all Englishmen to denounce a traitor, and well you know it, sir."

The day was warm and sunny and on every hand as they rode were signs of prosperity. Since the uprising many years ago, there had been peace in England. A peace tinged with unease, but nevertheless precious after the misery of his younger years, thought John. Why then on such a day did he feel the cold tingle that aroused in him the instincts of a threatened animal? That they had only scratched away the surface muck was almost certain. Were he and Jeffrey right in what they were doing? For the rest of the ride to York, John Weaver said little and thought much.

And when he had taken his leave of Jeffrey in the stable-yard of the tavern, the cold tingling in the small of his back persisted, nagging and warning him to have care.

Hurriedly he left Harry's letter and parcel of goodies with the old servant at the school door, convincing himself it was not right to disturb the lad's lessons yet knowing full well he dare not run the risk of being allowed the offer of a half-holiday for him.

What John Weaver had to do must be done secretly. Whatever the outcome of this day's events Meg's boy must never have wind of it. John could not know that had he asked to see the lad, he might have been shocked to learn that Master Weaver was playing truant again

and in line for yet another whipping for his misdeeds.
It came almost as a relief to John that Master Sykes was
laid sick with his stomach and whatever knowledge he
might have been inclined to give would have to wait.
Was it not the hand of Providence, he wondered, as he
crossed the Minster Yard, that had baulked him that
day? Were there things best not known?

Kit Wakeman was alive and living in York it was true,
but he had made no move to meddle in the affairs of
Aldbridge, or to show curiosity about the boy he had
fathered. It could well be that Wakeman wanted to forget his past and leave well alone.

Dare he then, thought John, leave him unmolested,
knowing almost certainly that he was a traitor to his
country? He would have to make up his mind which
was of utmost importance; the happiness of Anne and
Harry, or his duty to Elizabeth Tudor. He could not be
true to both, of that he was certain.

Could he tell his fears to Anne? Men said that trouble
shared was trouble halved. But Anne was his to protect
and he could not ease his own conscience by burdening
hers. And what would Jeffrey council. In Jeffrey's heart
still was a hatred of Kit Wakeman and John knew what
answer he could expect before he had even asked the
question.

John Weaver had forgotten the prodding finger of
Fate. Forgotten it at least until he rounded a corner and
saw Kit Wakeman. There was no mistaking him. He
had changed little in the years between. His breeding
clung to him still and the assurance of his bearing had
not altered.

Here was the man he thought had died by the axe at Tyburn. Before him still tilted in arrogance, was the head that once he could have sworn had rotted stinking above London Bridge. He had known for some time that Kit Wakeman was not dead, yet to see him again, even at a distance, made John puke. His every instinct was to run after the fellow and thrash the life out of him—a pleasure that once he would have given much to do, and because of his lowly station in life had been denied to him.

And yet he stood transfixed, watching as Kit Wakeman passed within a few paces of him and lifted the latch of his door. Nor had Fate finished her capricious game, for running down the narrow alley that led into the yard came a figure that made John Weaver think that some mysterious hand had turned back time.

She ran with feet that seemed to dance on the rough cobbles, her hair falling about her face like a sun-kissed web of palest gold. It seemed that the ghost of Meg was running towards the figure of Kit Wakeman, for if it was not Meg then it was her living image he was watching.

"No there, Mistress Beth!" called a young ragamuffin as she passed. "Your father's back and I'll tell him where you've been again!"

John let out a sigh of relief. He had not imagined the fleeting figure, for the child had seen her too and he had called her Beth. It had not been Meg's unhappy little ghost he had seen. At least his reason was left to him, and now it urged him to be gone.

He wanted to run from the spot and seek a place to hide. Some refuge where for a few quiet minutes he

could collect what remained of his shattered being. For
now he knew the meaning of the warning that had
tingled down the bones of his back. He could not be
sure of the answer and only one man could give it to him.

The little maid had entered the house of Kit Wakeman, or Master Cedric Woodhall as now he was known.
She could only be his daughter, and if that were so, John
knew beyond the shadow of a doubt what he must do.

"Tell me, Jeffrey," he asked as they neared the sweet
peace of Aldbridge, "what was the name of Harry's
little wench? You remember, the one you teased him
about the day you rode into York with the tithe money?"

Jeffrey Miller thought for a while. Sir John had acted
more than a mite strange on the journey home. Something, he thought, did not ring true. That Master Sykes
had been sick in his bed was all the knowledge he had
been willing to impart. Sir John, thought Jeffrey, was
holding back for reasons best known to himself. What
he had found he certainly was keeping to himself, for the
time being at least, and there was nothing to be done
about it.

"I believe, Sir, Diccon, said her name was Beth," he
answered, reluctantly, "and I think, were the truth
known, Harry wants to wed her."

"Aye."

John Weaver slouched in his saddle. He had delayed
asking the question for as long as he could. Now he
wished he had not. He should have listened to the warning that had whispered in his ear and told him not to
meddle. But he had asked the question and the answer

he had received was the one he had not wanted to hear.

Kit Wakeman had a daughter called Beth and Harry had been eager to be back to York. When the first hot blood of manhood surges through a youngling's veins, it is nature's way that he should go wenching; it was the order of creation that he should.

But did Harry, out of the whole of York city—nay, from the whole of God's wide world—have to fall in love with Kit Wakeman's daughter? He had debated, thought John, what was to be done about Wakeman's treachery, and he had been uncertain. But now the matter did not rest between himself and his conscience. He was no longer free to make the choice.

Harry, it seemed, was set on marrying Beth. With Kit Wakeman still alive such a marriage would be impossible. Kit Wakeman must die, then no one would know the intolerable burden that now weighed so heavily on John's unhappy soul. But even with Kit Wakeman dead, it would not be the end of the matter. Save for a miracle, Harry must now be told, thought John, what he and Anne had sought for so long to hide for all time.

John's heart cried out against she who had been the root cause of so much of his grief. She who had fled Scotland for France but had landed instead in the north of England. She whose implication in the plot to seize Elizabeth Tudor's throne so long ago had incited Catholics in England to rebel and in so doing, destroy the innocent with the guilty. Sweet little Meg had died trying to warn Kit Wakeman that the Catholic plot had been discovered.

Why, thought John, should Mary Stuart be allowed to

live on? Why did she still breathe good English air? The majesty of queens, however guilty, John knew to be inviolate and Scottish Mary, though captive, was still a queen. Was she not, for all that, party to far greater treachery than many who had died a traitor's death?

But John Weaver could not know of the house at Chartley where Mary Stuart now held court or of the Staffordshire brewer whose obliging beer kegs hid correspondence that passed from Mary Stuart to Spain and France; or of messages of hope and expressions of loyalty that came by way of the beer cellars to the Scottish queen.

Nor could he have heard of Master Giffard the Catholic renegade who played a double game, or of Master Phillips who deciphered those messages before he passed them to Sir Francis Walsingham. Few knew that time was running out for the wilful beautiful woman whose indiscretions were to be her undoing for on that soft July evening by way of a letter to Anthony Babington, Mary was busy signing her own death-warrant.

Of one thing John was certain as he rode home in the gathering twilight. To whatever depths he was willing to descend to protect those he loved from pain, Meg's love-child could not have his Beth. Station or breeding meant nothing now. Harry could not be allowed to marry his own half-sister.

CHAPTER SIX

HALF the shire was in York for the Michaelmas fair. Apple-wives, red-cheeked as the fruit they sold; candle-makers with fat candles of yellow tallow for the poor and elegant wax tapers for the rich; cheese-makers from the plenteous dale of the Swale and horse-sellers from the northern Marches.

All these and many more thronged into Market Street as housewives bought in their stocks for the approaching winter and city merchants haggled with farmers over the price of a bushel of wheat or a sleek young goose.

And amidst the din and clatter, the stench of the gutters and jostling, sweating bodies, Harry held Beth's hand tightly, afraid they would be swept apart in the heaving throng.

"You will wear the ribbons I bought you, Beth, to remember me by?"

"If I dare, Harry. But I shall sleep with them beneath my pillow," she hastened, "always."

"A handful of ribbons. It seems a poor offering, sweet-heart."

"No, I shall treasure them, and keep them for ever."

"The next gift I give you will be a gold ring."

"Aye?"

"You doubt our love, Beth?" Anxiously his eyes sought hers. "You will wait for me?"

"There is none other for me."

"But you will wait?"

Her fingers tightened round his.

"Yes, my darling, I will wait."

Slowly they left the rabble behind them, walking over the cobbles of the street of the spur-makers and feeling in their faces the fresh autumn-scented wind that blew from the wide river.

"I will write to you. I will write often. Can you read, Beth?"

Strange, he mused. He ached for the sweet creature who walked at his side until it throbbed like a pain inside him, and it amazed him that wanting her so desperately, loving her so completely, he did not know this one small thing about her. But their talk had not been of the common-place. Reading was of no importance when there had been golden summer days and soft sunsets and Beth's gentle lips near his own.

"I will write to you, love, though how you will ever receive my letters I do not know."

"There will be a way, Beth. Jeffrey often rides into York, and Diccon will get word to you, too, if he's not gone back to sea. And there will be times when I shall be able to visit the city myself."

"With the dark days of winter coming, and the roads bad to travel?"

Viciously Harry Weaver kicked a stone. This was not right! He had wanted to leave school. Now that day had come, and he was close to manhood. But to leave his desk behind meant that Beth would be half a day's ride from him and not just a street away.

Of late, his life had been tempered with the thrill of

anticipation; that he might turn a corner and unex-
pectedly find her there, smiling as though she knew they
would meet. Now he was going home to Aldbridge.

"Beth, love," Harry took her small unhappy face in
his hands, oblivious to passers-by. "There will be a way.
I am determined to speak to my father about our
marriage. I will be side tracked no longer. My father
will only want my happiness, and when your father sees
you are making a good match I am sure he will not deny
us."

"Aye, my father. He has been mighty strange of late.
I wish I knew what secret he keeps in his heart."

"He has no secrets, Beth. A man wants what is best for
his daughter; it is right it should be so. And I'm glad he
does not want you to marry the coppersmith's apprentice."

"He wants me to marry no one, yet. I must wait. That
is always what I must do—wait. And for what?"

"Maybe he wishes you to wait until you are seventeen or eighteen. Some parents do not favour early
marriages."

"No, Harry. It's something more than that. It is as if
my father knows something I do not. He is like a man
who stands by the quayside, waiting for his ship of
treasure to come in."

"I don't understand you, Beth."

"I don't understand myself, and I don't understand
my father. But there is something, somewhere, that rules
his life and he is waiting for it to happen. And when it
happens I will be able to marry, and into my true
station. What *is* my true station, Harry? I am a clerk's

daughter, and nothing will change it."

"You are Harry Weaver's beloved. One day you will be the Lady Elizabeth—*my* lady—and the mother of my children."

"Do you really believe that?"

"I *know* it. And I know I must meet Diccon with the horses at Micklegate Bar at noon, and it is long past that time. Why do we have to part, Beth?"

"They say parting is sweet, for it makes the heart love more."

"Could you love me more, little sweeting?"

She shook her head, unable to speak for the tears that threatened.

They were walking now across the Ouse bridge and the September breeze that blew upriver gently lifted the long fair hair of the girl, and tumbled the boy's unruly curls, whispering sadly of autumn. And soon would follow the dark days of winter when roads were quagmires and men travelled as little as they need. And come the spring, the youngling thought, would his Beth have forgotten him or be given in wedlock to another? The thought was intolerable.

"Beth love, let's away to the priest. Somewhere in this city of churches there is one man of God who would wed us this day. I weary of waiting and I fear I will lose you. Marry me now, darling."

"No, Harry." She shook her head miserably. "Something in me forbids it—yet. When I come to you it will be with the blessing of our parents—yours and mine."

"So you do not want me?"

"Oh, Harry. I want you." A tear slid down her nose

and plopped on to her tilted chin. "I want you so much it hurts inside me. But I have faith in our love, and if it is to be, it will be given to us. Have faith, as I have?"

"Faith? Hell, faith is cold comfort when a man's whole body throbs for a maid! Do you really know how much I love you, Beth?"

She nodded her head.

"I know, for I know how much *I* love *you*."

"Then what is keeping us? Some strange fancy you cannot explain? Some notion that you are not of my station in life? Some treasure ship that has not yet left Utopia?"

She looked at him through eyes bright with tears. She loved him to desperation yet within her the inborn instinct of a woman urged her to wait. For what, she did not know. She knew only the time had not yet come.

"I love you," was the only answer she could give him.

"I might have known I'd find you here!" Harry Weaver elbowed his way to where Diccon stood in a small circle of men. "Cockfighting, and the horses and packs standing neglected! I'll wager you've got money on it, and all!"

Diccon grinned, his eyes not leaving the prancing birds.

"That I have. I stand to win an angel if the game-cock kills."

To the shouts of the watchers, the two birds slowly circled, suddenly jabbing with their spurs or tearing with vicious beaks at eye and head. And when the blood-lust was on the big game-cock and he had clawed and torn his opponent into insensibility, the knot of men dispersed and Diccon cheerfully collected his gold angel.

"By the Lord, there's money to be made with a pair of good cocks. Help me Harry if I don't get some for myself. That big bird made mincemeat of the other."

On the feather-strewn cobbles the white cock lay jerking in its death-throes, bloody and blinded; fit for nothing but the cooking pot.

"And where have you been till now? Noon, you said, and it's past two of the clock. We'll have to ride like the wind to make Aldbridge by night-fall."

"Aye, Diccon. I was saying goodbye to Beth."

"Ah, well." Diccon swung himself on to his horse. "There's plenty more fish in the sea."

"What do you mean?" Angrily Harry turned on his friend. "I want to marry Beth. I'm going to marry her!"

"Nay, Harry, have sense. Beth is not for you, and you know it. You've had good sport, man. Leave well alone!"

Grim-faced, Harry Weaver jerked his horse's head and jabbed his heels into its flanks.

"I tell you I'm going to marry Beth."

"Hell, man. You've not got her with child?"

"No I have not! I've not even bedded her, though God knows I've wanted to. Beth isn't like that."

"I know it, Harry. I know it. Don't jump down a man's throat. I only said . . . "

"Leave it, Diccon!" Tight-lipped, Harry stared ahead. "I'll tell my father as soon as I get home about Beth. I've tried to before, but he can be mighty evasive when he's a mind to. I'll make him listen to me tonight, though."

"Aye, and like as not he'll tell you he's got a nice young wench all lined us with her marriage settlement in her hand."

"Then they'll have to drag me to the church door!"

"By God, I do believe you mean it, friend'"

"Of course I mean it, Diccon. There's only one maid for me, and that's Beth Woodhall. And if my parents won't stomach it, then I'll wed no one!"

"Does it matter all that much? You've got lands and wealth coming to you, Harry, and you've got to father a son to pass them on to. Be honest. One maid is much the same as the other with the candle blown out!"

"Beth will bear my sons. *Beth, or no one!*" Harry Weaver hissed, and for the rest of the journey home, he rode in stony silence.

"Where is my father?"

"He is out."

Anne Weaver set a plate of meat before her son.

"I know he is out, mother, but surely he knew I was coming home?"

Anne smiled indulgently at the petulance of youth.

"He knew it, and expected it two hours gone. What kept you both? Some mischief, I'll be bound."

"But I wanted to speak with him."

Things were not going as Harry had planned. He had been impatient to tell his father about Beth. The whole way home he had rehearsed in his mind what he would say. Now his father had gone out.

"You may speak to him when he returns. What is so important that it won't wait?"

"He has business with Father Sowerbye and the Parish Chest."

"And is the Parish Chest more important than me?"

"You are being impudent, son. The poor must be taken care of. The poor cannot wait."

And *I* cannot wait, thought the youth. I cannot wait and I will not!

"I want to get married, mother."

"So?"

"As soon as possible. Now! "

"Now?" A furrow of anxiety creased Anne Weaver's brow.

"There's a maid in York—Beth. We love one another."

"You've not wronged her, Harry?"

"No, mother. I want to wed her, not just to bed her."

Anne let out an audible sigh of relief.

"You have treated her always with respect?"

"Always, I swear it! "

"I am glad."

Kit Wakeman had not treated Meg so gently, she remembered. But then, thought Anne, Kit Wakeman had not wanted to marry her. He had been pledged to the Markenfield wench. Meg had merely been—what was the word—a doxy. Anne shuddered inwardly. It was a cruel word, but that was what Kit Wakeman had made Meg. Thank God Harry had not harmed *his* little maid.

"She is beautiful, mother."

"All lads think their sweetheart is beautiful—or should do."

"And she is modest and very shy. Why, I was weeks just gawping at her as she walked past me in the street."

"Calf-love!"

"Maybe it was. But I like Beth, as well as loving her. Can you understand?"

"Yes, son. I can understand."

Harry balanced his fork on his forefinger, his meat untouched.

"She has a funny little laugh and her nose tips upwards."

The fork clattered to the table.

"Hell! I love her so, and it makes me mighty miserable!"

"Nothing worth having is easily got, Harry."

"You *do* understand, mother." He looked up in amazement. "You're not going to forbid me?"

Anne shook her head, smiling gently.

"Tell me about her?"

"She lives in the Minster yard—near the school. I used to see her often and wish I dare speak to her. One day, after the Easter holidays, she dropped her basket and I ran to her help. It started from there."

"Great oaks from little acorns . . ." Anne prompted.

"Aye. We used to meet in the Abbey gardens. There weren't many people there. We met in secret, always.

"It was good when her father went to London. Her father's a clerk and sometimes must travel on the Queen's business."

"Then she is of a respectable family?"

"Aye, mother."

"And God-fearing?"

91

"I think so." He hesitated. "I have not met her parents. Her father is strict and she would not take me to her home. Not even when her father was away."

"Has she told them about you, Harry?"

"No, she has not." Anxiously the boy twisted the stem of his goblet in his fingers. "Her mother wishes her to be pledged to the coppersmith's apprentice, but her father forbids it. I think he wants better for her, so there's a chance for me, don't you think?"

"Ah."

"Mother. Don't go all mysterious on me! I'm a fair match, am I not?"

"I think so—but then, I'm your mother."

"And you'll not find a wife of your own choosing for me?"

"I did have one or two little maids in mind . . . "

"But you have not yet spoken?"

"No, son. We have not spoken."

"Then I have saved you a deal of trouble, mother, in finding a wife for myself." The boy grinned, relieved beyond measure that the first hurdle had been taken. "You'll be on my side when I speak to my father?"

"We'll see." Anne smiled. "We'll see."

And Harry knew then that as far as his mother was concerned he was home and dry. Ever since he could remember, "We'll see," usually meant "Yes."

"I am not hungry, mother." Harry pushed aside his plate. "I think I will take a walk, and see Goody."

He picked up a russet apple, biting his firm white teeth into the creamy flesh.

"How is Goody faring?"

"She is well. For an old woman, she is well. She often talks of you, Harry. You are her special favourite. But then, when you've a mind to it, you could charm the birds from the trees."

Dear old Goody. She had promised, if she was able, to plead his cause. It seemed to Harry that she had done so.

"See that Goody has wood enough for the night," Anne called, "and fill her water buckets from the well!"

But the door had already slammed.

Anne smiled indulgently. No more partings. The roisterous lad whose presence seemed to fill the great house with sunlight and whose absence made it seem empty as a tomb was home for good and with a wife in mind, at that.

Beth? Perhaps her name was Elizabeth, Anne mused. It would be good to have a daughter in the house again, and God in His wisdom knew the manor house was big enough and empty enough for two families.

How good it would be to have a modest little maid to sew and gossip with when the men were about the estate. How fine to have grandchildren tumbling about the place. Anne Weaver smiled a sad, wry smile, Grand-children? They would be her great-grandchildren, wouldn't they?

"Master Harry does not want his supper," said Anne as Molly answered the ringing of the bell. "Place the meat in the dole-cupboard for the beggars," she ordered, "and when Sir John returns, tell him I am in the store-room by the apple loft."

Picking up her skirts, her eager feet fairly flew over the polished treads of the wide staircase. The little storeroom was a special place for Anne—a memory room. In it she kept her precious things—Meg's rocking cot that Harry had used; the cedarwood chest full of baby clothes; Harry's little carved oak chair.

Dropping on her knees she opened the chest. It was filled with both sad and happy things. Meg's tiny bonnets, soft lambskin rugs, finely woven blankets, Harry's little jackets, so soon outgrown and the swaddling bands of fine linen.

Anne remembered the night she had knelt on the stone floor of the farmhouse where they had once lived. She had been plain Anne Weaver then and not a lady of title. Meg had been alive, and until that night they had known utter happiness together.

"Get her wed, and soon," Goody had said, "for Meg is with child."

Anne opened the chest that night and cried until her heart must surely break. Now she was happy. It might not be long before the tiny garments must be taken out and used again. Impatiently, Anne fretted for her husband's return.

She did not expect, when finally he came home, to be met with such evasion, such indifference to her joyful news.

"The lad is too young," he had said at first. "He is only seventeen."

"Diccon is pledged, and he is younger," Anne pointed out.

"What Jeffrey and Judith wish for their son is no concern of ours; nor is it a yard-stick for our own behaviour to measure up to."

"We could meet the maid, John? She seems to be well-reared. Harry is eager to marry her. Is it so wrong to marry for love alone? Did not our love-match turn out to be a good one?"

"Aye, Anne, it did. But for Harry it is different. He must marry one of his own station."

"John!" Anne was shocked by the words she could hardly believe she had heard. "Is this the young penniless weaver I married who talks in so lordly a fashion? Have you so soon forgotten the humble station into which *we* were born? By God's Holy Mother, I'd give much at this minute to be a housewife again and scrub my own floors and milk my own cow! What has got into you, husband?"

John had not forgotten, nor ever would, but Anne's excited greeting had knocked him off balance. Always at the back of his mind he had known this day would come and now that it had, he was at a loss to deal with it. Would it be best to tell Anne now that Harry could not marry Beth, or would it be best to wait a while and hope that a few months' parting would help quench the flame that now burned so fiercely? Whatever happened, Harry must never be told of his true parentage. John must have time to think; but how, with Anne's stubborn insistence to contend with and Harry's quiet determination to overcome?

He had thought of telling Jeffrey of the sorry mess, but had decided to let well alone. Now, something would have to be done, for what had appeared to be a boyish fancy that might flame brightly and die quickly was now a matter to be reckoned with seriously.

Harry could not marry his half-sister. That was the only thing in the whole miserable business that was clear. Would that Kit Wakeman had died on the executioner's block. Would he had never assumed another identity and lived to father a daughter. Why had Fate guided that daughter to Harry? By God, thought John, he would give much to see Kit Wakeman dead now!

Dead? That awful thought hit John Weaver like a douche of ice-cold water. With Beth Woodhall's father dead, things would be much clearer, for then no one need know, save perhaps Jeffrey. Jeffrey would know about Beth, and that Kit Wakeman was not dead. It would only be a matter of time before Jeffrey would perceive of the truth of Beth's parentage. Would Jeffrey hold his tongue for Meg's sake, or would his conscience forbid it?

But even with Kit Wakeman dead, dare he hold his peace? thought John. What of the children of such a union? They would be tainted—dare he risk it? Dare he let Harry and Beth marry? Could he live with his conscience if he did?

"Let me think about it, Anne. Marriage is a serious step, and not to be taken lightly. *We* waited, you and I. If Harry's love is so strong, surely it will stand a little time for thought? I will think what's to be done, Anne. Trust me?"

That night, John Weaver did not sleep, for sleep does not come easily to a man who has gone to his bed with murder in his heart.

PART TWO

1587

CHAPTER SEVEN

IT WAS a fine February morning—the kind that hints of spring. Elizabeth Tudor had ridden out from her palace at Greenwich to enjoy the rare sunshine, but the elation she felt on her return was soon to be sobered by the dour faced minister who awaited her.

"Well, Walsingham?" she asked. "What causes this most urgent intrusion on our privacy?"

She threw down her gloves and riding crop and held her long, slim hands to the glowing coals.

"Your Grace, Lord Talbot has arrived with news from Fotheringhay."

The royal shoulders lifted and stiffened.

"Yes?"

The Queen stood immobile, head erect, her eyes staring at the intricate carving of the mantel.

"He rode with all speed, Majesty."

Sir Francis Walsingham addressed his stumbling remarks to the royal back, for which small mercy he was almighty grateful, Elizabeth Tudor did not speak.

"The bells, your Grace. Do you hear them? They ring out from every church in London. The people are giving thanks for your deliverance."

"My deliverance from what, Sir Francis?"

"From your enemies, your Grace. The Queen of Scotland is dead."

"*She is what?*"

She spoke the words slowly, spitting them out like well-aimed bullets.

"Say that again!" she said, and turned to face the trembling man.

"Mary Stuart is dead, your Grace. By the axe. Shortly after nine of the clock yesterday morning."

"By God, but bad news travels fast!"

Walsingham gazed into the amber eyes that slowly narrowed till they were slits in an inscrutable face. The spots of rouge on the queen's cheeks flared red on a face that had blanched to paper-white.

"On whose orders and by whose authority did the Queen of Scotland die?"

"By Royal Warrant, Majesty."

"I know nothing of this."

"The warrant you signed and gave to Master Davison."

"I sign many warrants. I sign warrants until my wrist aches!" She took a deep breath as if to steady herself. "And a warrant is but a scrap of parchment without my seal. Who fixed my seal to it?"

"I presume, your Grace . . . "

"Presume, little man? On whose authority do you presume to interpret the Queen's wishes?"

"Your Council of Ministers, Madam, understood that it was your wish . . . "

"My wish, Walsingham? My ministers *understood?* By our Lord, they have placed me in a pretty pickle with their *understanding*. They could not have done better had they given me the axe to sharpen!"

Sir Francis Walsingham shifted uneasily, waiting for

the storm to break; hoping that it would. He had seen Elizabeth Tudor before in the throes of cold passion, spitting out words as a snake spits venom. A ranting woman he could deal with, but the icy Queen before whom he stood, frightened him to the tips of his itching toes.

"She was your enemy, your Majesty. She desired your throne and connived at your death."

"She was my cousin and of the blood royal. She was an anointed queen."

Walsingham stared at the muted colours of the fine Persian carpet and remained silent. He knew that above all else, Elizabeth Tudor desired the death of Mary Stuart. The Scottish queen had been a constant bait to English Catholic plotters. For nineteen years she had lived under the protection of the Queen of England, though many would have called her a prisoner. And Elizabeth had been reluctant to free her and afraid to keep her.

Mary Stuart, whilst in England had been a spur to those who desired to see a Catholic ruler on Elizabeth's throne. But Mary Stuart, if banished from England's realm would have been a greater danger. And so she had been shifted from house to house, a burden on England's peace of mind, and a burden on those who were chosen to be her gaolers.

While the Scottish exile lived, there could be no peace in the land, and Elizabeth had known it. Now, when they had given her what she wanted, she stood accusing and calm. Too calm. For a moment she stood still and white as a marble statue.

"Leave us," was all she said.

When the sound of the retreating footsteps was gone, Elizabeth Tudor picked up her skirts and fled, passing startled servants as though she had not seen them. On feet of terror she sped along the gallery, and up a small twisting staircase that led to her bedchamber. She did not want to be alone. She dare not be alone.

"Get out!" she hissed to the ladies who were laying fresh silken sheets on the royal bed.

Leaning her back on the thick oak door she gulped air into her heaving lungs in long shuddering gasps. It had almost seemed that the phantom of Mary Stuart had followed her near-hysterical flight, brandishing an axe dripping blood, calling her name with every footstep. "Elizabeth! Elizabeth!"

"Blanche!" the Queen called, her voice cracking in terror. "Blanche Parry!"

"I am here." Mistress Parry stood by the closet, a dress of black hanging over her arm and black silken weeds trailing from her hand. "You'll be wearing these?"

"You know, Blanche?"

"Aye, by way of the groom who rode with Lord Talbot."

"Damn him! I'll have his loose tongue cut out!"

"It's common knowledge, your Grace. The bells of London have been proclaiming it this last hour."

"I didn't want her dead."

"You wanted her dead, but not by your hand."

Blanche Parry took liberties. In the whole of Elizabeth Tudor's kingdom she was the only one who dared.

"She plotted against me."

102

"Aye, it was strike, or be struck."

"Yes, Blanche, that's it. It was her or me, wasn't it?"

The pretence of the audience chamber was over now, the acting done. Here, in the privacy of her bedchamber with faithful Blanche to mirror her conscience, there was no need for falsehood.

"By her own hand she condemned herself. The letters she wrote to Babington proved it beyond doubt."

"Beyond doubt," confirmed Mistress Parry.

"He would have killed me—he who had my confidence, enjoyed the privileges of my court. God, the times when I think back to when he was within the thrust of a dagger from me. I trusted Master Babington. I knew he was a Catholic, but I held my peace. I made the mistake of thinking that above all else he was a good Englishman."

"And now his poor mangled body rests under six foot of English earth."

"Aye, and all who plotted with him. What have they done with—*her*—Blanche?"

"They have put her in a lead coffin, somewhere secret in Fotheringhay. None are allowed in and none allowed out of the castle."

"How was she? Did you hear?"

"They said she died almost gladly. And she died like a queen."

"She was determined to be a martyr."

"She was proud, at the end."

"Aye." Elizabeth Tudor watched as Blanche Parry's deft hands smoothed out the folds of the mourning gown.

"Those Stuarts. They didn't know how to rule, but by God, they know how to die!"

"Jane Kennedy was with her. And Mistress Curle. She prayed right up until the end."

"Popish prayers."

"She willed her English throne to Philip of Spain."

"She has no English throne! The throne of England is *mine*. I was fathered by a Tudor, and in wedlock, too, despite what Rome says!"

There was silence in the room for a while. The Queen of England stood by the window, gazing down at the broad sweep of the Thames, trying desperately to control the terror that took each limb and shook it as though it were made of jelly.

"Did she cry out?"

Elizabeth did not want to know but she could not refrain from asking the question. Her slender hand fondled the smallness of her neck.

"She just said 'Sweet Jesus,' when the axe missed and hit her head. They said the second blow took her."

"No!"

"They said her lips continued to move in prayer for full fifteen minutes after they had cut her head off."

"Stop it, Blanche Parry!"

"And know you, when the axe-man took hold of the head and lifted it high, the hair came away in his hand. She was wearing a wig, your Grace!"

"Be quiet, damn you!" The words rose to a scream of hysteria. "Be quiet!"

Flinging her face into the soft folds of the bed Elizabeth Tudor wept.

"God! God! God! Why did she make me do it?"

She pummelled the pillows with fear-clenched fists, her heels beating frantically into the soft mattress.

Quietly Blanche Parry left the room. It was done now, and nothing could change it. The only medicine for her beloved mistress was tears. Left alone, she would cry until she was sick. Blanche Parry understood.

At lonely Escorial, the palace that seemed more like a monastery than the home of an Emperor, they told Spanish Philip of Mary Stuart's death. He had gone first to his chapel to compose himself and pray for guidance; to call on the same God that Elizabeth Tudor prayed to, and with much the same purpose of mind.

Now he sat alone. Now it was not so much a question of what was to be done, but when?

Elizabeth Tudor had killed a queen—a Catholic queen. Mary Stuart had been anointed before God and could not, by all the laws of chivalry be tried by any but her equals. But she had been sentenced to death by a handful of earls and lords, and with Elizabeth Tudor's blessing.

The gnarled fingers drummed angrily on the wooden arms of the chair. Damn Elizabeth for the bastard she was. Devil take her for a jezebel! Her ships had harassed his galleons, plundering Spain's treasure for English coffers. The pirate Drake had made the Spanish navy into the laughing stock of the world.

By God, thought Philip, bitch that she was, Elizabeth Tudor had made a fine ruler. Would she had only professed the true faith, she would have had no equal, save perhaps for himself. But now she had thrown down the gauntlet and it must be picked up. It would fall to him, Philip of Spain to rid the world once and for all time, of heretics. He believed he had been given life by the Almighty for just that purpose and from his bounden duty he could not swerve.

But he was getting old and already his purse was strained by the troublesome Netherlanders. And Elizabeth had had a hand in *that,* too, sending her lover, Leicester, with troops to help the Protestant rebels. Elizabeth Tudor had, he was sure, been spawned by the devil for the sole purpose of tormenting him.

He remembered, long ago, the day he had first seen her. Once, when he had had hopes of ruling England from Mary Tudor's bed, Elizabeth had been summoned to court. There had been no love lost between his once-wife, Mary Tudor, and her sister. Mary, God rest her, had been a true Catholic, whilst her half-sister Elizabeth had been reared to Protestantism.

Poor, barren Mary. How dull and lifeless she had seemed beside the glowing girl, dressed demurely in virgin white. By God, in his younger days thought Philip, he'd have bedded her and gladly, aye and given her many sons.

She had stood demurely before him, her amber eyes cast down and she had mocked him silently. Mocked *him,* Philip of Spain. It had been a mistake to hint at marriage with her when later Mary had died. Elizabeth had flung his proposal back in his face and straightaway run to the bed of her horsekeeper, no doubt.

Now, the whole world watched and waited. It was

Philip against Elizabeth; heresy against God's truth. The affairs of France were too involved to tangle with Elizabeth's stubborn little country, despite the fact that Mary Stuart had once been Queen of France. No, it was left to him, Philip, to avenge the murder of the martyred queen and claim the throne she had willed to him. It was his duty before God.

He would send a fleet so mighty that men would ever remember Philip's vengeance. He would grind the English pride into the dust with his heel. He would whip the whore Elizabeth through the streets of London in her petticoat and with her the damned seamen who had plagued him for so long. He would burn and pillage and cast out for all time the rotten canker in the breast of England.

And God would reward him.

The priest who travelled from York to Ripon stopped in Aldbridge to break his fast and the news he brought with him was so terrible that Father Sowerbye had sent for Sir John Weaver that he too might hear it.

In the manse kitchen the servant who rode with the priest regaled the gory details of the Scottish queen's beheading to the serving maid who straightaway sped with it to Agnes Muff and Molly in the manor-house kitchens.

Barnabas the Fox-catcher offered his services to Father Sowerbye and for a groat pulled long and cheerful on the bellrope of St. Olave's church, bidding all who heard it to come and kneel in thanksgiving for the deliverance of Queen Elizabeth from her enemies.

But that night, when prayers had been said and the Almighty thanked for his goodness, John Weaver's heart held no elation.

"It will mean war with Spain," he said.

"War?" Anne's busy needles stopped their clicking. "Why should it mean war?"

"The King of Spain must avenge her death. The world will call him chicken-hearted if he does not."

"It is none of Spain's business." Anne was indignant. "The Queen of Scotland made no pretence of coveting Elizabeth's throne. She got her just deserts."

In Anne's heart were bitter memories still of the uprising of northerners who had sought to put Mary Stuart on the English throne. It had brought devastation to the county, but mostly, to Anne, it had been the cause of Meg's death. Often, in the years that passed, Anne had wondered why she who had caused it still lived on, whilst Meg lay dead and buried. She had rejoiced when Kit Wakeman who had betrayed Meg had lost his traitor's head at Tyburn. Would, she had thought, Mary Stuart had died with him.

"It was God's judgment on her," Anne insisted.

"The Almighty had already sent a sign," declared Goody Trewitt from her warm seat in the ingle. "Before her death the guards at Fotheringhay saw a bright light. It flashed before them three times and turned night into day, it is said."

"That is nonsense, Goody," John retorted, sharply, "and you know it."

"I know that when one of the blood royal dies, a star falls," said Goody, unperturbed. "It is always so. I have lived long and seen many things, John Weaver. Did I not tell you on Mark's Eve that it would be so? Did I not see the passing of a queen?"

Triumphantly, she hitched her shawl around her shoulders.

"And I forbade her to go again," John said, eager to change the subject.

Goody *had* seen the spirit of one of regal bearing and they had thought it was Elizabeth Tudor's death it had foretold.

"And I shall see to it that Father Sowerbye minds what I told him, and locks the churchyard gate, this year," he said with conviction.

"Locking the churchyard gate won't stop what is to be," said Goody, comfortably. "Last Mark's Eve the Almighty called Mary Stuart to her rest. This year—who knows?"

"None will know, Goody, for none will keep vigil," John Weaver insisted. "Hush your old wives' tales. What concerns us now is far more frightful. We must pray in church tomorrow that God will protect the right, for only God can help us if Philip throws his great ships at our shores!"

"God and *Englishmen*," said Anne quietly. "It will take more than Philip of Spain to lick our sea-dogs."

"I pray you are right, Anne."

John Weaver rose and carefully lighting a taper walked to the door of the manor house and lit the porch lantern. It would guide Harry home from the mill, he thought as he looked at the stars that sparkled frostily in the cold February night.

"Sweet Jesus, let there not be war," John whispered.

He knew what Anne's womanly reasoning had failed to grasp. Wars meant killing and always it was young hot blood that was spilled. They had lost Meg. Were they now to give Harry?

CHAPTER EIGHT

THE soft May dusk had merged into a sky of black velvet and the first star was shining high over Weaver's Oak when John reached the crossroads and settled himself to wait. His thoughts tossed hither and thither like a leaf on a rain-swelled beck. What he was about to do he knew only too well. How he could bring himself to do it was another matter.

If only, he thought, the young were not so exuberant. Why did they have to live as though each day were their last and tomorrow but a tantalising promise?

"Wait," he had cautioned when confronted by both Harry and Anne. "If your love is true as you say, then it will stand the test of time."

"And for what, sir, do we wait? You will not even agree to meet Beth!"

John sighed into the darkness. When a lad nears eighteen his blood runs hot and his curiosity hotter.

"What has set you against the maid?" Anne had demanded. "Has your new station in life made you so high-minded that you forget what it is to love?"

Anne's remark had hit John like a slap in his face. How could she think he had forgotten their humble beginnings? How often, when the cares of the manor and the people who looked to him for protection and justice had irked and troubled him, had he wished for the simple life again? To be back at the farmhouse with nothing more to worry him than a perverse wind that blew wood-smoke into Anne's immaculate houseplace was what he often longed for with all his heart.

To return after a day in the hayfield or a morning spent in the weaving loft and find Meg dreaming by the hearth was sometimes, even yet, his own private dream of Utopia. But he had so much now to be grateful for. Elizabeth Tudor had settled rank and wealth upon him and in so doing had, at the stroke of a pen, turned Harry from a bastard love-child into the son of a nobleman. The Queen had made Harry's future secure and in the wording of the title deeds had made it well clear that Harry was the son of John Weaver of the Manor of Aldbridge.

It was right that Harry should marry and father sons to love and care for Aldbridge as John did. But the one maid in all the world he could not take was the one he wanted above all else. And now Anne had added the weight of her stubborn personality to Harry's insistence, for Anne did not know Beth's true identity. He could tell Anne, decided John. She would be hurt and disappointed but she would understand.

But how could they then tell Harry why he must never marry the maid he loved with all the passion in his bursting young heart? To do that would be to take his world and crash it into smithereens at his feet. How did you tell a proud youngling that he may not marry his half sister? And having told him, would he understand that for the whole of his life you had lied to him and deceived him only to protect him from the slur of bastardy and the taint of a traitor father?

Would he ever understand their motives or trust their word again? For what Harry, or Anne for that matter did not know, was that Cedric Woodhall, Beth's father, was really Kit Wakeman. And Kit Wakeman was at the best a spy for Sir Francis Walsingham and at the worst a Jesuit sympathiser who played a double game and lusted for revenge.

If only he could be sure, mused John, that Kit Wakeman *was* playing the traitor, he could do what must be done with a clear conscience. But he had no proof of Wakeman's treachery. Instinct alone did not license cold-blooded killing.

The soft air rustled the tender young leaves of the oak tree he had planted long ago to protect Meg's secret grave. Why had he, thought John, chosen this spot to meet Kit Wakeman? Was it to be Divine justice that the man should meet his end over Meg's resting place, if rest she did? Would John know then that Meg's uneasy soul could at last have her lover?

"One day, in another life, I will come again and find you, Kit," she had whispered in her dying delirium.

Was *he*, debated John, to be the instrument of that justice? He did not want to take Kit Wakeman's life. He had never spilled blood. Could he, in all conscience, destroy the man who had fathered Harry? Could he, if Kit Wakeman's tongue was stilled for all time, let Harry have his way and marry Beth? Who then would know, save perhaps Jeffrey, that Harry and Beth were of the same blood? Could he let them marry? *Dare* he?

Why, he fumed, had he despatched Jeffrey to York with the letter?

"Give it to Master Sykes for delivery. You must not confront Kit Wakeman yourself," he had ordered, for Jeffrey's heart was steeped in hatred still for the man who had betrayed Meg and returned from the dead. Jeffrey would kill him with his strong broad hands, and do it gladly, with no more compassion than he would feel for the sticking of a pig.

When at last he could no longer sidetrack Harry's demands to marry, John had played for time.

"You are but a youngling, Harry. It is better you should wait until you are twenty-one before taking a wife," he had insisted.

"That is not fair!" Harry had passionately retorted. "They will marry Beth to another, and I shall lose her."

"Maybe it is not fair, lad, but it is sensible. I waited until I was four-and-twenty before your mother and me were wed."

"But only because the law demanded it," Anne interposed. "You were apprenticed to the weaver in Feltergate. You could not marry until you had served out your time."

"And were we any the worse for waiting, Anne?"

"I'll allow you we were not," she conceded, "but Harry does not need to wait. He has a fine home to offer his bride and wealth to support her with. He will inherit Aldbridge one day and need sons to help him tend it and pass it on to, when God wills it."

"You look too far into the future, Anne. There may

114

be nothing for Harry to inherit, if Philip of Spain crushes England."

"And why not, in that unlikely event?"

"Aldbridge would be given back to the Wakemans. They were staunch supporters of the old faith."

"There are no Wakemans left, and you know it, John Weaver. Old Sir Crispin died in exile in France, and we all know what became of his only son!"

Anne's glib remark jolted John. He had forgotten she did not know Kit Wakeman had not died. He must have more care. Anne was nobody's fool.

"It would be given then to one of their blood. It is miraculous how long-lost kin appears when there are pickings to squabble over."

"John, what has gotten into you? I'll swear you invent trivialities to suit your own purpose, and you so square and honest a man!"

But John had remained adamant. He knew full well that Harry journeyed into York as often as he could and when he could not, letters were carried by any man who might be travelling in that direction. This he could not forbid. He had merely asked for and been reluctantly given, Harry's promise that he would not marry without his parents' blessing.

And now there was an uneasy peace, but who knew how long, aye, or how soon it would be before youth must have its way. Harry was but flesh and blood, like the next man. There may come a time John knew, when Harry might go his own sweet way regardless of his promise. If that time came, it would be as well if there were none who could cruelly disillusion the lad or demand the annulment of his marriage. If it did not come and the fire that raged so fiercely in Harry burned itself out, then nothing would have been lost by keeping back the truth.

It had been that line of thinking that had led John Weaver to this night. What he would say to Kit Wakeman when he came he did not know. He knew only one thing with absolute certainty; that at all costs Harry must not suffer, *would not* suffer, and to that end John had vowed, he would kill if necessary. It was no use praying to God for a way out of his troubles. John had straightened his conscience with the Almighty; now the rest was up to himself. And didn't the good God aid those who aided themselves?

John's hand tightened on the hilt of his sword. Calmer now, he knew what must be done.

The man approached with the sinister stealth of a witch's cat and took John Weaver unawares, standing before him without speaking so that immediately he had gained the advantage.

"So you have come, Master Wakeman?" John said at last.

"I am Cedric Woodhall, but I have come."

John could feel the contempt in the voice of the man who stood beside him in the darkness.

Angry at being taken by surprise and stung by the indifference of his adversary, John Weaver flailed in to the attack.

"Then you may turn round and return from when you came. I have business only with Kit Wakeman. I know no Cedric Woodhall."

"No?"

"But I'll tell you before you take your leave, Master Woodhall. Kit Wakeman is a seducer, a betrayer and a Papist!"

John heard to his satisfaction the quick hiss of indrawn breath.

"He seems to be a thoroughly bad lot. It may be that I remember him from the past. Were not his estates given by Harry Tudor's bastard to a clodhopping farmer?"

"They were," John refused to be goaded, "after he and his father had forfeited them for treachery!"

"After they were taken from him by a usurping queen who stoops to murder to keep what she holds!"

"I would not call it murder to behead one who plots against the Queen of England."

Kit Wakeman had given John the opening he wanted and he pressed home his advantage.

"All those who seek to overthrow a crowned queen must pay with their lives for it. Did not you yourself come within an ace of death many years ago for the same thing, Kit Wakeman?"

There was no reply.

"How did you buy your freedom, Kit Wakeman? What did you give in exchange for your life?" John taunted.

"Damn you, John Weaver—"

"It was not your head that festered beside young Norton's on London Bridge. Which poor wretch died in your stead?"

John Weaver had the advantage now and he pressed home his attack.

"How did you cheat the axe-man, Kit Wakeman? Did you accuse another poor innocent as you accused Meg? Is there nothing you would not stoop to, to save your worthless hide?"

"You'll regret this, John Weaver. I swear it on Mary Stuart's martyrdom!"

"So! You show your hand. You tell me where your true loyalties lie!"

God, thought John, if I could but see his face!

It seemed the Almighty had heard. Slowly the soft night clouds that covered the moon began to drift away.

"Aye, and I care not if you know it!"

"You are brave, Master Wakeman! I could denounce you for the traitor you are!"

"You could, John Weaver, but you will not, or before the words have scarce left your lips the whole of the riding will hear of the pretty little deceit you play. Remember, I too know of the babe your innocent Meg bore!"

"By Christ Jesus you should! You fathered him!"

"Aye, and it seems strange that one of my bastards stands to inherit my lands!"

If he had had any doubts, they were at that moment dispelled for all time from John Weaver's mind. Now all fear of conscience was gone. He looked at the arrogant face before him and knew he *wanted* to kill Kit Wakeman.

John took a deep breath. He wanted to be calm and savour the moment. He wanted to kill in cold blood.

"Do you know where you stand, Kit Wakeman?" Slowly John spoke.

"No, and I care not!"

"You stand by Meg's grave. And do you know why I sent on you to attend me here?"

Kit Wakeman answered with a shrug of his shoulders.

"I brought you here this night to kill you."

Lovingly almost John Weaver's fingers wrapped themselves round the hilt of his sword.

"You and who else to aid you, old man?" The taunt was almost laughed into John's face.

The dagger Kit Wakeman whipped from his pocket was sent spinning from his grasp. He flung round to face the adversary who had attacked him from behind. John Weaver's sword hissed from its sheath.

"Leave him, Jeffrey. He is mine!"

"Not if I get to him first, Sir John!"

With a look of settled hatred on his face, Jeffrey Miller stepped from the shadows, his thick stave grasped at the ready.

There was no escape for Kit Wakeman. Even as he threw himself for the shelter of a tangle of bushes, Jeffrey sent him sprawling. With one leap he was by his side, towering above him. Viciously he jabbed the heel of his boot beneath the upturned chin of the fallen man.

"One move, Kit Wakeman, and I'll crush your gullet as happily as I'd crush a rat in my granary!"

He emphasised his words with a sudden downward thrusting of his foot and knew the satisfaction of hearing the man he hated gasp in pain.

Slowly he eased his boot a fraction and turned his stave downwards, poising it a foot away from the writhing man.

"Or will you have my stave through your belly? I care not which it will be."

Deliberately and with satisfaction he spat into the upturned face.

"Hold, Jeffrey!"

For the space of a second, John Weaver had been thrown off his guard. He had thought Kit Wakeman to be unarmed, for only noblemen were allowed the privilege of wearing a sword. He had not reckoned with the concealed dagger that had been in Wakeman's hands with the blinking of an eyelid.

How Jeffrey had known of this meeting, John could not begin to guess. He only knew he was grateful that at this time Jeffrey stood beside him, strong and steady as an old castle keep.

Kit Wakeman was right. John knew himself to be getting old. Old and sometimes weary. When he had been possessed by hatred and temper he could have killed. Now, he was not sure. He stood, sword in hand, above the man that Jeffrey held secure.

"Well, Sir John?"

The steel-tipped stave was still poised. It seemed that only superhuman will-power on Jeffrey's part was holding it back.

"Steady, Jeffrey. I'll take him."

John looked down into the bulging eyes of the half-choked man and all the arrogance was gone from them. Now they glinted fear in the cold moonlight.

"Kit Wakeman, I know you for a traitor to your Queen and country." John spoke the words slowly. "You run with the hare and you hunt with the hounds. I could kill you now and have to answer to no man for doing it."

"God rot you, John Weaver!" The words came in a strangled croak.

"Mind your manners, Master Clerk!"

Jeffrey's boot crunched again into the soft throat.

"You speak to Sir John Weaver. Give him respect and tip your cap when you address the nobility." Again the boot thrust. "Go on, man, say it. *Sir* John!"

Kit Wakeman tipped his forelock.

"*Sir* John!" he screamed between gasps of pain. "*Sir* John!"

"That's better, traitor," said Jeffrey, with mock gentleness.

"Kit Wakeman, I accuse you of treachery." John knew he must play his trump card, and soon, for Jeffrey was lusting for blood. One slight movement from Kit Wakeman was all that was needed to send the spiked stake tearing into his guts, or a heavy boot to shatter his windpipe and break his neck.

"You spy for Walsingham yet you are in league with the Jesuits."

For the first time alarm sprang into Kit Wakeman's eyes and John knew with absolute certainty he had hit on the truth.

"You visit mass-houses, not to spy as you would have Walsingham believe, but to pray and conspire with those who would kill Queen Elizabeth!"

"No, I'll swear it is not so! My word on it, Sir John!"

"Your word, Kit Wakeman, is not worth the spittle in my mouth!" John shook his head wearily. "I came here this night to kill you. Had not Jeffrey arrived, I would

121

have done it, make no mistake about it. I wanted your blood to water Meg's grave, but your bad blood would have fouled it. Once, Meg loved you and you fathered her child. That child is now *my* son. He will inherit one day what should have been yours, and he will never know or own you. For Harry's sake, I will spare your life."

"Nay, Sir John!" Rage and disbelief echoed in Jeffrey's protest.

"For Harry's sake, Jeffrey, *and* Meg's," John said quietly. "And anyway, yon dog is not worth one sleepless night, and you know it."

"Then what's to be done with the louse?"

"He will leave the country. He is not fit to breathe good English air." Slowly John returned his sword to its sheath. "This is what I will do, *Master Woodhall*. Tonight, I will write to Sir Francis Walsingham. I will tell him who you are, and what you are. There will be a price on your head and every true Englishman's hand will be against you. Tomorrow, at daybreak, Jeffrey will take that letter to London. He will be there this day week, if not sooner. You have just six days to leave these shores. Where you go, I care not. Only do not return!"

John's adversary knew he was beaten.

"I have no choice," he said, grudgingly.

John nodded to Jeffrey. "Leave him be."

Slowly Kit Wakeman struggled to his feet, his hands to his injured throat as though, even yet, it was not safe from Jeffrey's impatient hands.

"I would have killed you, dog," hissed Jeffrey. "I'd

have done it gladly and thrown your carcase on a stinking dunghill. And mark my words, it will be the best thing in life I ever do to carry word of your treachery to London." With derision he spat on the ground. "Six days to leave the country? I warrant I'll do the ride in far less. And watch out for your worthless life, Kit Wakeman, for if I meet you on the roads, I'll throttle you with my bare hands. Steer a course clear of Jeffrey Miller, or your life won't be worth a groat if I clap eyes on you!"

"Get you gone, Kit Wakeman," John spoke with reluctance, " 'lest I change my mind. And the devil take your black soul!"

There was a small silence, broken only by the sound of hurrying feet.

"I shall be back, *Sir* John Weaver. Make no mistake, I'll be back. When Philip takes this land and burns all heretics, I'll kindle your pyre with my own hands. Philip will give me back what the whore Elizabeth took from me!" The voice croaked harsh from the distant shadows. "On Mary Stuart's sweet soul, I'll be back with King Philip!"

"A pox on King Philip!" Jeffrey's stave hurtled hissing into the darkness.

John let out a sigh of relief, glad that the night's work was all but over.

"That was a waste of a good stout stave, Jeffrey," he smiled.

Jeffrey shook his head.

"I'll never know what prompted you to spare him, Sir John." He grinned. "I'll pick up my stick when I set out, tomorrow."

"You will go to London for me, Jeffrey? Can you be spared?"

"Aye, Sir John. There's little work at the mill until the corn harvest is in, and Diccon can take care of his mother whilst I am gone. I'll go, and willing."

Slowly they began the walk home.

"I'll never know how you guessed what I was up to, Jeffrey, but I've never been so glad to see a man in all my life. He'd soon have had the advantage of me, were the truth known. What made you come?"

"It was the Lady Anne. She arrived at the mill, breathless from running, and nigh on sick with worry. I thought of the letter I had carried to York and set out to look for you. I heard your voices in the darkness. From then on, it was simple."

"You are a true friend, Jeffrey. God will reward your goodness."

"Nay, Sir John." The miller modestly shook his head. "I remember Meg."

"Aye," John shook his head. "Sweet little Meg of the heartsease. I could not have killed Kit Wakeman this night, for she truly loved him."

Jeffrey was silent.

At the manor house gates, John held out his hand.

"I thank you, Jeffrey, for tonight you saved me from doing murder."

"Then I am right sorry, Sir John," Jeffrey grinned. "I'll be with you at first light. You'll give me the stallion to ride? He goes like the wind, that brute."

"At first light, Jeffrey, the letter will be ready." John

rubbed the back of his neck. "Now I must face my lady wife. I fear I'll be in for a scolding."

"You'll tell her?"

"No. I'll convince her that her fears were groundless. There's no need yet for her to know."

"And what of Harry?"

"Harry?"

"Aye, sir. Harry and Beth."

"Then you know about Beth Woodhall?"

"I've suspected it since I first clapped eyes on Kit Wakeman in York."

John shook his head, sadly.

"I might have known it. I thought this night that with Kit Wakeman dead, I might have permitted the match. Even with him out of the country, I could have allowed it, but it would not be right, would it?"

Jeffrey did not speak.

"I mean, I thought at one time I could live with my conscience if I permitted the marriage, once Kit Wakeman was taken care of. I'm in a cleft stick, Jeffrey. Either I let them marry, which would be a grave sin, or I tell Harry why he may not have his little maid. Either way it can only lead to heartbreak."

John spread his hands in a helpless gesture.

"And what of the bairns of such a match, eh, Jeffrey?"

Again there was a silence. Jeffrey Miller knew he must neither help nor hinder in the matter. It was for Sir John and his conscience to battle out between them.

Presently he spoke.

"You will do what you think is best, Sir John. Whatever you do, I will hold my peace. And I will pray for you," he said.

John shook his head, fighting back the emotion that threatened to choke him.

"God bless you, Jeffrey Miller," was all he could say.

PART THREE

1588

CHAPTER NINE

TALK had it in the taverns in York that Spanish Philip had amassed a fleet so great that its like had never been seen before. But to the people of that inland city, ringed on three sides by stout, well-kept walls and protected on the other by the broad waters of the Ouse, it was easy to boast of Martin Frobisher and joke about King Philip's poor beard.

"They say 'twill never grow again after the singeing Drake gave it in Cadiz, last spring."

Nevertheless, there were those who were not so confident. In the Abbey gardens, their favourite trysting place, Harry and Beth walked hand in hand.

"Will there be war with Spain, Harry?" Beth asked, anxiously.

"Sometimes I fear so, little love. My father says it must come."

"You will not go?"

"I must, Beth. My family has much to be grateful for to Queen Elizabeth. We cannot accept her bounty and deny her our loyalty."

"What does your lady mother say?"

"I have not told my parents, yet, that I intend to fight. When the time comes, if it comes, Diccon and I will tell them, and be away together."

"You will come back to me? You'll take great care of yourself, my darling?"

"Yes, little Beth. Nothing, not even Spanish Philip will keep me from you."

"I will pray for you and I will think of you every minute of every day."

Tears filled the blue eyes that gazed adoringly into his.

"There now, love. I have not gone yet. I may never need to go. Do you think I *want* to leave you?"

Beth shook her head.

"Then dry your tears. The worst has not happened yet. There are far more things to worry about than the Spaniards. You, my sweet. I awake some nights in a cold sweat, dreaming your mother has married you to Giles."

"That will not happen, Harry, I promise you. I worry, too, about your father. He is still firm?"

"Aye. Wait he says. Always it is *wait.*"

"Then we will wait, Harry. And besides, it has not been so bad since my father left. At least we can meet now, without fear, and you are welcome in our home."

"Have you money, Beth?"

"We manage well enough. My mother is a fine seamstress and we can pay the rent, and buy fuel."

"I told my father I intended to visit you today. He asked how you were both faring and sent you these."

Harry fished into his pouch and dropped three sovereigns into Beth's hand.

"Your father is a fine man, Harry. We cannot refuse his bounty for we cannot afford to. It is mighty good of him to worry over us, though why he should, I cannot imagine."

"You are right, Beth. I am blessed with fine parents.

That is why I cannot understand my father's insistence that we cannot wed. He thinks nothing of rank, so why we must wait for two more years, I do not know."

Beth wiped away her tears, smiling bravely.

"We will wait, Harry. Our love is strong and we are young. Nothing will part us, I promise you."

"Not even if your father suddenly returns, and forbids it?"

"I think he will never return, Harry. Why he left, I do not know. He was always a strange man, and it was never easy to love him. I pray for him at night, for all that, and my mother prays too."

"Your mother? I thought you had never seen her so happy?"

Beth gave a little giggle.

"Nor have I. She prays to St. Uncumber to keep him away from her!"

The tension was broken and the threat of Spanish revenge that loomed constant over England was forgotten. The lovers drew together.

"Tell me, Beth?" demanded Harry, his lips close to hers.

"I love you," she whispered, standing on tiptoe and drawing his face close to hers so that she could kiss the tip of his nose and his eyelids. "I love you. I love you."

"Sweet little Beth."

He kissed her urgently, roughly crushing her mouth beneath his own, his whole body crying out for her as he strained closer. He had given his promise that he would wait, and that he would conduct himself like a gentleman towards Beth. He loved her and he wanted to marry her, and two more years of waiting seemed to stretch beyond Eternity. Sometimes he wished he did not love so much; it would be easy then, to take her.

Beth recognised the urgent trembling in his body, and drew herself away. No, said her eyes, and Harry understood.

"God, Beth, when the time comes you will cry out for mercy from my love!"

She shook her head, womanly wise beyond her years. "Will I?" she teased. "Oh, will I?"

And then they linked hands and ran like children through the long grasses, warm in the June sun.

Walsingham's spies were in. They reported that a massive fleet was ready to set sail against England. It was small comfort that only a year before, Sir Francis Drake had destroyed thirty-seven Spanish ships in Cadiz harbour, or that Philip's trusted Admiral, the Marquis of Santa Cruz, had died. More ships had been speedily built and another admiral had been found.

With fanatical haste Philip had assembled another Armada. And now, the spies said, galleons and great-ships were at the ready and galleasses rowed by three hundred slaves and store ships and transports strained at their moorings in the summer sun.

The Archbishop of Lisbon had blessed the fleet whilst soldiers and sailors confessed and were absolved, confident that they were the chosen instruments of God.

And in Elizabeth's England, merchants and shop-keepers and yeomen grown fat from years of peace knew that war with Spain must come.

Sir Francis Drake had a fine fleet at the ready. But England's defences were broken and useless, and men toiled day and night to repair the neglect of complacency. From each town and village the levy-men converged on London and blackmiths and armourers sweated to forge the weapons of war.

In forests far from London, the thud of axes and the crashing of great oaks provided yet more timber for yet more men-of-war. In boatyards around the coast, ships were repaired, then tarred and caulked and freshly painted.

"This is costing me greatly," fumed Elizabeth Tudor.

With her fleet on a constant alert, and sailors eating their heads off, even the Queen was impatient for it all to be over and done with.

"They say," said Anne Weaver, "that the Vavasours have felled most of the oaks on their estate, and given the timber to the Queen."

She was walking with her husband in the orchard, her fingers entwined with his. Anne had never, she thought, remembered so beautiful a spring or the trees so thick with blossom. Behind them the stone of the old house was mellowed by the late afternoon sun, the tiny glass panes in the mullion windows shining warm and secure.

But how secure was this peaceful house? How long might they be able to keep it, now that Philip of Spain was gathering his might to hurl against England? It seemed strange, Anne mused, that nothing is ever so precious as when it seems it will be lost.

"The Queen must have more ships, Anne."

"But the Vavasours are Catholics. They attend prayers in the English church then straightaway pray in their own way in their own chapel. Why should they help a Protestant Queen?"

"Why should Lord Howard take charge of the fleet? He too is known to stand true to the old faith," John begged the question.

"Then do you think, John, that Catholics will fight for Elizabeth, or will they rise against her when the Spaniard comes?"

"I don't rightly know, love, but when I look at these green pastures and the great forests of oaks; when I see men well contented and most times well fed; when I see the great bounty of this fertile place and remember the years of peace and the justice all men enjoy, then I think when the times come all who live in this realm will forget all else, save that they are Englishmen."

"Did they remember they were Englishmen when they rose up against the Queen? It was because of that rebellion Meg died. Mary Stuart came to these shores and begged the Queen's protection. And in return men flocked to her side and York's fair county knew misery because of it."

"Mary Stuart is dead now, Anne."

"Aye, at last she had paid the price, but something of her lives on. It will take more than the lead coffin that lies guarded at Fotheringhay to keep her spirit tight. Oh, she is dead, John, and what has come of it? Spanish Philip must now avenge her death!"

"There, love, don't fret yourself." John patted Anne's

trembling hand. "It will take more than Philip to bring Englishmen to their knees."

"But why, John? Why? Sometimes it seems to me that we live in a vast cave and always there is the echo of Mary Stuart, somewhere above our heads, threatening and taunting."

"Then think of her as that. Mary Stuart is but an echo, now. She died true to her faith. Let her rest in peace. Nothing can harm this land, let alone an echo."

"I pray you are right, husband."

"I would wager everything I own on it."

Anne squeezed the beloved hand in hers.

"You are a great comfort to me, dearest man," she said. "Take care of yourself?"

Anne Weaver worried about her husband. Of late, he had seemed preoccupied. It hurt a little that he had not confided his worries to her, but always, John had his reasons.

It may be, thought Anne, that her husband was worrying about Harry, though why on earth he should, only the good Lord knew. Harry wanted to wed—he'd be a fop of a fellow if he did not. Why should John refuse to even meet Beth Woodhall, or talk to her parents?

John was a nobleman now, but he had never risen so far above himself that he ever forgot his humble beginnings. Why, if Beth could make Harry a good and loving wife, could they not be allowed to marry?

John knew that Harry was away like the wind to York on every possible occasion. What was to be gained in delaying? Harry had been true and unwavering these two years past. Beth was no passing fancy.

"I had a despatch from the Council in York this morning, Anne."

"I saw a Queen's Messenger ride up. Is there trouble about the tithe money?"

"No, it is not money. The Queen wants soldiers. I am to send four levy-men and arms to London."

"Who will go?"

A tremor of fear ran through Anne's bones.

"I will call a meeting at the church tonight. I think there will be no need to press men into service."

"Do you think that Harry—?"

"I would be proud to think he would serve his Queen."

Anne shivered. She had known it must come. Above her head the echoes sang. Suddenly her safe, warm world was a cold and lonely place. First Meg. Now Harry?

"Harry is a gentleman by the Queen's grace. It is his duty, Anne."

Duty? Harry was man enough to fight and perhaps to die. Why then was he denied a wife? A surge of anger ran through Anne. Her obstinate chin tilted.

"Then I'll tell you this, husband. If our lad fights and proves his manhood and God gives him back to us, he shall wed his Beth!"

She drew a shuddering breath.

"I have loved and obeyed you always, John, for it has been easy for me to do it, but on Meg's memory I swear that when Harry returns he shall take what wife he chooses!"

The sunset song of a blackbird piped clear in the soft

air and the lowing of the cows in the milking shed seemed familiar and safe. Yet John's world turned a cartwheel and landed broken at his feet.

Anne, though never openly opposing his refusal to let Harry marry, had not sided with him. She was anxious to see the lad wed and she loved him with an intensity that would deny him nothing. If only he could tell her the truth of the matter.

"Trust me, Anne love?"

Tears of rage and frustration splashed down Anne's cheeks.

"*He will wed Beth!*" she choked, and picking up her skirts, ran for the house.

"Sweet Jesus," whispered John, "help me to do what is right?"

On the green outside the manor house gates, the whole of the village had assembled to wish God-speed to the levy-men. They had prayed in St. Olave's church and those who wished it had confessed to Father Sowerbye and received his blessing. The Council of the North had demanded four men of Aldbridge but many times that number had volunteered and straws had been drawn to select the ones who should go.

Harry had claimed his privilege as a nobleman and Diccon declared that already he was a seasoned sailor, and Martin Frobisher, the Yorkshire sea captain could not sail without him. Gideon, John's blacksmith had drawn a short straw and Luke the archer, whose skill with the crossbow was the pride of the riding had triumphantly drawn another.

"You will want to ride by way of York, Harry?"

"Aye, father. We will pick up the other levy-men there and travel with them to London."

Sadly John looked at the lad. Doubtless the few hours he waited in York would not be spent in the taverns but in saying farewell to Beth.

John had supplied horses from his stables. They should all ride out proudly, he insisted.

"Leave your mounts with the ostler by the Ouse Bridge, Jeffrey and I will collect them later." John handed a purse to Harry. "This will care for all your needs on the journey. Look well after Diccon and the lads."

"I will, sir."

"And remember your prayers," whispered Anne.

Harry smiled, his eyes already on the road. He felt elated and at the same time sick in his stomach. He wanted to fight, God knew, but he wanted so desperately to come back to Beth.

"Good St. Olave," he whispered, gazing at the old church. "Keep my Beth safe until I return."

He had never known the delights of Beth's sweet body. Maybe now, he never would. He had given his word to his father that he would respect her maidenhood and he had struggled to keep his promise. If only once, before they parted, he could take her, he thought, he would ask for nothing more, but give his life then into the good Lord's keeping.

By Anne's side, Goody Trewitt wept unashamedly, and Judith Miller stood bravely, her tiny daughter in her arms. It seemed that the whole of the village was trying to hold back time.

Harry dug his heels into his horse's flanks. There was nothing now to be gained from delaying. Fondly his eyes embraced the village that was suddenly so dear to him. He tipped his cap in salute to his parents.

"God bless you all," he called, and was up the hill and away.

By the crossroads he pulled hard on the reins of his mare. Perhaps one look back?

The leaves on Weaver's Oak whispered a benediction as he stood there and the clumps of heartsease that grew beneath its shelter seemed to lift their tiny faces to wish him godspeed. There was a sighing in the branches of the young tree, as though Meg's lonely spirit yearned out to her son.

"I will be with you."

The words were caught on the summer breeze and borne into oblivion, from whence they had come. But Harry Weaver heard them.

There was nothing now for England to do but watch and pray. Around the coast great bonfires had been built, ready to blaze out a warning as soon as the mast-tips of the Spanish ships showed above the horizon, from which ever direction they should come.

In churches, for the first time in many years, Anglican, Catholic and Protestant prayed together, and Jesuit priests stayed close to a bolt hole. Those who had yearned for years for a Popish ruler had searched their hearts and found England more dear.

That the defeat of a Catholic invader would spell the

end of their hopes to worship in their own way had not deterred them. They knew that a victory for Philip would bring a revenge to England so terrible that the Spanish Inquisition and Mary Tudor's still remembered hell-pyres at Smithfield would seem like a May Day romp.

If Elizabeth Tudor had doubted the loyalty of her recusant Catholic subjects, she found her fears to be groundless.

"God bless them,' she had whispered, and straightway granted the Vavasours permission to hear the Mass said in the privacy of their chapel.

The long hot days of haymaking sped past and June drew to its close. There had been no word from the Aldbridge levy-men.

"I worry about Goody," said Anne as she counted the great cheeses made from the early-summer flush of milk. "She will not eat. When Goody Trewitt refuses her victuals she is mortal sick."

"Goody is getting old," said John.

"Not so old that she should puke at food. Why, she has often joked that so long as the good Lord lets her die on a soft feather bed with a chicken drumstick in either hand, she'll go happy."

"Perhaps you could tempt her with a dish of syllabub," John ventured.

At least, whilst there was Goody to fuss over, Anne stopped for a brief spell, her worrying over Harry.

"Goody is too old now to live alone. She just sits there and says her rosary all day. It's as if she were sick of this life and fled back to her nunnery days. She must come to the manor and live with us, John."

John welcomed the idea. Often Anne had declared that the old midwife must not spend another winter alone in her tiny almshouse.

"I think if you insist, love, Goody will offer little resistance this time."

The busier Anne was, John knew, the less time she would have for matters that were now in God's hands.

John had been right. Goody meekly bundled up her sparse belongings and without a backward glance, followed him to the manor house. Settled comfortably in a chair she took out her rosary again and stared into the empty hearth.

"What ails you, Goody?"

Anne set down the mug of milk the old woman had refused.

"You pray as though the troubles of the whole world rested on your shoulders."

"I pray for my sins, Anne Weaver."

And sins she had a-plenty, thought Goody. The sin of disobedience, for one. Why had she defied John Weaver? She should have not gone to the graveyard on Mark's Eve, for despite the locked gates, she had found it easy to enter.

Anne had been right. We are none of us the better, she had said, for knowing God's will. Would she had not been there, Goody brooded, when God had made his will known. Would she had not seen that awful vision of carnage. Had not the great astrologers predicted long ago that the year 1588—this very year—would be one of utter disaster?

And for her wilfulness, she, Goody Trewitt, had been rewarded with a glimpse of it all. Shadows ghosting about her like the souls of the damned, screaming at Heaven's gates; swirling mists of devastation, and pain in which nothing had been clear but one thing.

He had stood there amongst the lost souls, his head thrown back in defiance, and a smile on his lips. She had not known rightly whose face it had been for her eyes were useless as her old body, and blinded by tears of terror. But she knew without the shadow of a doubt that one of the young lads who had set out so gallantly to war would not come home to Aldbridge.

It had been her one aim, these past years, to live long enough to place Harry's first-born in his arms. She'd go then to her Maker in peace. But who was she to bargain with the Almighty? She had lost, she knew it. There was but one thing to do now; wait quietly for Death's angel.

"Sweet Mother of God, bring young Harry home," was her constant, desperate plea, and that night she spent on her knees, praying for the soul of the laughing youth God's finger had already marked.

And in the uneasy darkness, the men who stood watch at Staithes strained their eyes to the south to catch a glimpse of the fire that would tell them that the Armada had come, and mothers scolded their naughty children.

"Hush," they said. "Close your eyes and go to sleep, or the Spaniards will get you."

England waited, defiant and proud.

CHAPTER TEN

JULY blazed golden and the corn grew sturdy in the fields as though the angels smiled on England.

Goody Trewitt dozed and prayed and fasted in her chair.

Nerves twanging, Anne feverishly busied herself about the silent house, supervising the blanket-wash and the plaiting of rush mats.

"Damn them, will they *never* come?" she had fumed.

Ports were now barricaded and guns hauled to the coast. On York's stout walls the militiamen kept constant vigil. On the towering bars of the city, hawk-eyed archers stood at the ready. In the hearts of Englishmen, patriotism blazed like a sacred crusading flame.

"Perhaps they will *not* come," Anne dared at last to hope.

But then one of Drake's swift little scouting ships out from Plymouth had sighted them. They said Sir Francis and Lord Howard had been playing bowls and taken the news of the dreadful array of ships with calm indifference.

That night, the English fleet put to sea. That night the watchkeepers at Staithes saw Whitby's burning beacon and fear mingled with relief as they set light to their own waiting pile.

Now it had come. England stood solid, ringed round

by flame and hurled defiance at the might of Spain.

They had the news in Aldbridge on the first day of August, and hunchbacked Barnabas pulled with all his might on the bell-rope of St. Olave's church. There was no need to ask what the urgent irregular clanging of the bell proclaimed.

"It has come," whispered Anne and picked up her best hat with its defiant feather plume and ran with the rest to the church to pray.

There was little said in the manor house in the days that followed, so engrossed were those who lived there with their own private thoughts.

"Good St. Mark," prayed Goody, "for just this once, could you not have been wrong?"

John busied himself with the corn harvest, and rolled up his sleeves and wielded a sickle alongside his men as though his very life depended on it. For a brief while he could pretend that the old days were back again and he was cutting his own acre with Jeffrey, a boy again, at his side.

If he thought hard enough, he could imagine that Anne would soon walk across the fields towards him with cheese and fresh-baked bread in her basket, her body young again, her apron white in the sun. And she would complain loudly that Meg was dreaming by the hearth, and sick with love for Kit Wakeman.

John lifted his head, his eyes swimming for a second, unable to believe what he saw. But the figure in a fustian dress and white mob cap that ran across the stubble was not Anne's.

"Sir John, come quick! Come quick!" she called.

It was Molly, tears of joy running down her cheeks. "They are back safe, sir. Luke and Gideon are home!"

The reapers threw down their hooks, converging on the excited girl.

"Luke and Gideon?"

"Aye, Sir John. They are at the manor house now, and with such tales to tell!"

"Luke and Gideon?" Goody had whispered.

Just two of them? Then she had chided herself for her disappointment and thanked the Almighty for his mercy. Who then was it to be? Diccon or Harry—or both?

The great hall at the manor house hummed with excitement, for the whole of the village had gathered there to welcome home the younglings, and hear their proud news.

Anne and Agnes Muff had dragged out kegs of ale and filled flagons with barley wine and the joy was such that it seemed almost like Yule-tide.

"We saw the Queen," Luke enthused.

"She sat there like a vision," breathed Gideon.

And they told of proud Elizabeth, regal in white velvet sitting her white charger with the Earl of Leicester at her side, calling foul scorn on any who dared to invade her England.

There had been a great shout of love and loyalty from her troops that day at Tilbury.

"I'll swear before God, I'd have given her my life there and then," said Gideon.

John knew the feeling only too well. He had knelt before Elizabeth Tudor. To see her was to love her for all time.

Then news had come to the quayside at Tilbury about the fire-ships. Drake had sent eight blazing vessels bearing down on the crescent formation of the Spanish fleet as they lay at anchor off Calais.

"Imagine the Spaniards' dismay," exulted Gideon. "To see those ships, tarred all over and blazing, with their cannon spiked and loaded, white hot and exploding in their midst! They cut their cables and ran for it, with their Spanish tails between their legs!"

And those of them who could not escape the melee had faced the English guns.

"The Spaniards had no chance, the sailors told us." Flushed and triumphant, Luke took up the story. "They said our ships were like fleet greyhounds, snapping at the heels of great lumbering Spanish cows!"

So the waiting troops had been disbanded, the need for them gone. Doubtless Elizabeth had gazed at the mass of militia and levy-men and her Tudor soul had cringed at the great holes they must be eating into her privy purse.

"And what of Diccon and Harry?" Anne asked.

"We all made the journey safe to London, my lady. Then Master Harry and Diccon made for Tilbury. They were men of York they said, and wanted to sail with a Yorkshire sea-captain. The *Triumph* was victualling up; they said they would ask Captain Frobisher to take them on. It was the last we saw of them, madam."

"And you know no more about them?"

"No, my lady, save that they were in high old spirits when we parted.

John laid his arm round Anne's shoulders.

"They'll be all right, love. Already two of our warriors are home. In no time at all the young varmints 'll be back, demanding food and boasting of their exploits."

Anne smiled bravely.

"It would seem that the Spaniards have taken a thrashing from our sailors," she said.

"That they have, my lady. When Captain Drake had done with them they made a run for it into the Irish sea. They're scattered, mark my words, and still wondering what has hit them, I'll be bound. Sir Francis took the wind out of their sails, and make no mistake!"

"Then it seems this England is safe for all time," John smiled.

"Aye, husband. And she who was the cause of it all— I could find it in my heart now to hope she may rest in peace. Only let my lad come home safe, and I will pray for her soul."

"And Gideon and Luke? Shall we not all give thanks for their safe return, and ask the good God to send Diccon and Harry back, 'ere long?"

Anne held out her hand to John.

"That we shall, love, and right gladly."

And when they had all gone and the great hall stood silent and empty, Goody Trewitt sat alone, her barley wine untouched by her side.

"Give thanks for small mercies, Anne Weaver, but pray until Domesday, and it'll make no difference. One of the younglings will not come home."

A tear, hot and bitter, fell on the old hands that clutched the rosary, still.

"This day," said Anne as she forked bacon on to her husband's breakfast plate, "being the birthday of our Queen, I think we will roast the goose that hangs in the buttery."

John smiled.

"That we will, and I am glad you told me of it, for I awoke this morning with the feeling that there was indeed something I must remember."

"*Something,* John Weaver?"

"Aye, love. But there was another matter, also. It must be of small importance, though, if I cannot call it to mind."

Anne's face flushed, and then she saw the teasing in her husband's eyes.

"Did you think I could forget that this is also *your* birthday, my Anne?" He kissed the tip of her nose. "Close your eyes and hold out your right hand, for I have a pretty bauble for you."

"A pretty bauble? Why John, 'tis a pearl! "

The great jewel swung on its gold chain from Anne's trembling fingers.

"And do you not deserve it, Anne, after loving this poor oaf for nigh on forty years?"

Anne smiled, her heart thumping with joy.

"You have been an easy man to love, my John—and I thank you for my fine gift."

Excitedly, she fastened the pendant around her neck.

"John, love, this is going to be a special day—a very special day—for I feel it in my bones."

John understood his wife's meaning. Each day, since the return of Luke and Gideon, had started out to be a special day. The day on which Harry and Diccon would come home. Now they were into September, and the defeat of the Armada a well-established fact. But still the younglings had not returned.

"I think, Anne, on this your birthday, you might just be right."

Anne had ordered the goose to be killed and hung a week ago. It was, John knew, awaiting Harry's return. Today, it was certain Anne was about to try her hand at tempting the Fates. Today, they would cook the goose because today, Anne was sure, Harry would be home. She could pretend to honour the Queen's birthday. John knew what really lay in Anne's heart.

"I did hear it said, John, that pearls mean tears."

Anne fondled the creamy pendant.

"Tush, and away with your botherings! There are two kinds of tears Anne, remember that!"

"Mercy on us," gasped Goody Trewitt from her seat by the fireplace. "What's to do?"

From the kitchens came a shriek and a clatter. It seemed to Anne Weaver that all the pewter had crashed from the walls.

"Oh, come to the stableyard, my lady, do!"

The door of the small parlour burst open and a breathless Molly, waving her basting ladle, stood laughing and crying at one and the same time.

Anne found her hand being grabbed in a most unservant-like manner. On the kitchen floor a scattering of plates and dishes lay where Fat Agnes had dropped them.

"See, my lady!" Gasping with joy, Molly pointed to the open doorway. "The Saints be praised. He's home!"

Anne stood on the doorstone, unable to move, to laugh or to cry. Behind her she felt the pressure of John's hands on her shoulders.

"Harry," Anne breathed. "Oh, Harry!"

Leading a strange white mare, the youth walked slowly to where his parents stood. Pale-faced and dirty, his leather jerkin spattered with mud, he held out his arms to his mother.

"My lady," he whispered.

In a flash Anne was holding him to her, kissing his cheeks, fondling his hair, her tears now falling unashamed.

"Sweet Mother of God." She lifted her eyes to the sky. "Sweet lady, I thank you with all my poor heart."

Laughing like a young girl, she turned to John.

"Did I not say this would be a special day? Did I not say we would cook the goose?"

Overcome with emotion, John grasped Harry's hands.

"This is a day to remember, lad. My, but there'll be such feasting in Aldbridge this night. A goose, Anne? Please God and the village will eat us out of house and home! What say you to a right celebration, Harry?"

The boy shook his head.

"No, father."

Anne drew sharply on her breath, noticing for the first time the misery on Harry's face.

"What is it, son? What ails you? Have you caught a sickness? Why must we not rejoice?"

"We cannot, mother." The tired young face crumpled. "We cannot; for Diccon is dead."

The September twilight darkened the room where Harry sat staring into the blazing beech logs. They had set out, he and Diccon in such high spirits and had not believed their luck when Captain Frobisher had taken them on to the *Triumph*. There had been the small thrill of fear when they put to sea and joined the fleet at Plymouth. Aldbridge had seemed far away as they took their place amongst the ships that proudly flew the red and white flag of St. George. It seemed to Diccon and Harry that they were men amongst men, and to fight and die for Elizabeth was all they had ever lived for.

Harry had been glad that Diccon was beside him.

"Is it not good, friend, to feel the spray and taste the salt?"

And Diccon had shouted with mirth, for Harry had never felt so ill in his life.

"Sup a draught of sea-water, Harry. 'Twill soon cure the sickness," he'd said.

All his life, Harry thought, he'd remember the night of the fireships and the great barrage of English shot that poured into the cumbersome Spanish ships. And always Diccon had been there, laughing from the sheer glory of it.

"By God, Harry, there'll be such tales to tell in Aldbridge when we're home!" he'd yelled, above the noise of the battle.

Harry had not been so fearless as Diccon. Diccon had not puked at the sight of the gore that dripped from the scuppers and cannon hatches of the Spanish vessels. Diccon's face had not turned green at the sight of decks that ran red with Spanish blood. He had still been laughing when the *Triumph* had become detached from the rest of the fleet and found herself pinned against the coast, unable to make a run for it.

Four Spanish ships had closed in on them. It had been a musket ball from the *San Lorenzo* that had shattered his guts. And with his head cradled in Harry's lap, Diccon had smiled up at him right until the end.

"Diccon?" whispered Harry to the flames that danced shadows on the walls of the room. But Diccon was no more. There would be no more wrestling and fisticuffs in the meadows, no more whispered confidences, no more mischief together.

Diccon had lived a life-span in his few short years and had laughed even as the death-rattle had choked in his throat. And with Diccon, a small piece of Harry's heart had died too.

"Diccon?" he whispered again, but Diccon had gone for ever.

In her bedchamber, Anne Weaver decided against the plumed hat. It was not fitting to go to church this night decked out in finery. Selecting the shawl of fine black wool she draped it over her head. First she would pray for Diccon and then she would visit Judith and Jeffrey. There was nothing she could say or do that would help. Perhaps though, they would know she understood their grief.

The little stone church was deserted save for the woman bowed before the altar. Quietly, Anne knelt beside her and reached out to touch her with her hand.

"Judith?"

The pale face lifted and dry eyes, stricken with grief looked into Anne's.

"My lady?"

Anne's hand rested on Judith's. For a while they knelt together in prayer, shoulders touching, each glad of the other's closeness.

Presently, Anne spoke.

"There is nothing I can say, Judith that will help you and Jeffrey, but try to remember that I too have suffered as you are doing now."

Mutely, the sorrowing woman nodded.

"Sometimes I think the good God plucks our sweetest flowers for himself. Heaven will be the happier place Judith, for Diccon's laughter."

The pearl pendant lay warm on Anne's throat.

There are two kinds of tears, John had said.

This day, thought Anne, I have tasted both.

CHAPTER ELEVEN

"You say he took *two* horses?"

"He did, Sir John; the mare he brought back from London and the big chestnut." John Weaver's horseman was as puzzled as his master. " 'Have them ready for first light, William,' he said to me last night."

John could understand that Harry would want to be with Beth at the first opportunity. That he should take two horses pointed to only one thing. Harry intended to bring Beth and her mother back to Aldbridge.

John recalled Anne's words, flung bitterly at him.

"He shall have his Beth!"

Anne had meant what she said. Now, she was so happy to have Harry safely home she would immediately take his part. It was useless to look to Anne for support unless she were told the truth of the matter.

It was certain that Kit Wakeman would never return to England. With a price on his head, the risk would be too great. Wakeman would probably live out his days in exile as his father had done, and John felt not one tremor of remorse that he himself had been instrumental in causing that banishment. Kit Wakeman was no longer a danger.

All that now remained was for John to decide whether or not he could commit the grave sin of letting Harry and Beth marry. Jeffrey had given his word that whatever John decided to do, he would remain silent, and so far as John knew, Jeffrey was the only other person who was aware that Kit Wakeman was Beth Woodhall's father.

John walked slowly across the cobbled yard, feeling nothing of the crisp chill of the early autumn morning. If, he thought, before we are born we were granted just one wish, I would ask that I come into the world without a conscience. But his conscience was God-given and he had always lived by it. He could not change, now.

Perhaps, if he took a walk to the crossroads and stood by Meg's oak tree, she would help him, for Meg he knew, was wise now beyond all worldly imagination. Dear little Meg who had loved too well and too sadly. Was the child of her love to be hurt in just the same way?

Bellows in hand, Agnes Muff bobbed a curtsy as John walked through the kitchens.

"I will take a walk before I break my fast this morning, Agnes. Will you tell Lady Anne I will be back within the hour?"

Fastening his cloak around his shoulders, John quietly closed the door behind him. He had so much to be thankful for he thought as he walked across the dew-damp green and up the hill. His house was not steeped in mourning as Jeffrey's was.

The harvest had been a good one and now, for the most part, safely in. He had fodder enough for his cattle for the winter, a stout roof over his head and fuel in plenty. Many a man with much less would be more than content.

John quickened his step, eager to be beside Meg. That she would help him, he was absolutely certain.

The morning chill was off the streets of York when Harry rode beneath the great bar at Micklegate and into the city. His heart pounded with joy and anticipation; his spirits were high.

Last evening as he lay in his bed, he had become aware of the sheer joy of being alive. He had lived through days of danger so great that they would never be forgotten His life-long friend had died in his arms but he, Harry Weaver, had come home unharmed.

Against all this what had seemed to be insurmountable troubles had paled into insignificance. He loved Beth Woodhall and she loved him. It was as simple as that. He was a man now. He would thumb his nose at tradition. There was no law that said a man must marry into his own social class; it was merely a fact of convenience.

A man—his own father—could rise from the status of a weaver to that of a wealthy nobleman. No one worried about that. Why then should he not marry Beth? His father had asked that he should wait. It was most unlike him, but he had asked it. Now, Harry swore, he had waited long enough.

Master Woodhall had deserted his wife and daughter without so much as a farewell. Had he returned, Harry wondered? If he had, it would make no difference. There was much he could offer Beth and he would take on the devil himself, let alone Beth's disagreeable father, to get her.

Nothing had changed. Harry looked about him in sheer amazement as though he expected that the bloody battles fought around England's coasts could have altered this city. Beggars still stood on the street corners, showing their mutilated limbs and asking for alms. Farmers' wives sold butter and eggs as they had always done and apprentices in their blue smocks scurried back and forth on their masters' business, winking at serving maids who scrubbed doorstones with wisps of straw.

And Beth? Beth would not have changed. That night they had parted—its memory had sustained Harry when he had been homesick and afraid. The thought of her love had been a spur to him; had brought him back to her. Now she was just two streets away from his arms and nothing, he vowed, would part them again.

He saw Beth standing in the doorway of the little house in the Minster Yard. She looked small and defenceless. At first she did not see him, and Harry reined in his horse, willing her with his eyes to look up, savouring each tiny detail of her body whilst his heart thumped with happiness.

Then she turned her head, smiling a little as she saw him; suddenly shy.

"Beth," was all Harry could say.

She stood, radiant faced as he walked up to her, loving him with her eyes. And then they were in each other's arms, bodies touching; their lips meeting as though nothing would ever part them.

"Darling," she whispered. "My dearest love, you are safe."

"I will never leave you again," he whispered, his mouth scarcely leaving hers.

Beth pulled herself a little away from him and placed her fingers to his lips.

"My mother is sleeping. We must be quiet."

"She is ill?"

"Not any more, though a week back she called for a priest."

"Then you will both come home to Aldbridge, with me."

Gently, almost sadly, Beth shook her head.

"No, love."

"Yes, Beth. I have brought horses. I shall not leave without you."

Again his lips sought hers, urging her into submission.

"We must talk, Harry."

"What about?"

"About us. I—" She hesitated, her lips trembling, her eyes seeking his, imploring his understanding. "I cannot marry you, Harry."

Unbelieving he stared at her.

"You've not given your pledge to another?"

Mutely, she shook her head.

"Then why, my darling? Why?"

"There are—reasons."

"What reasons?" Harry tilted her face in his hands, forcing her to look at him. "You are not . . . ? That night Beth, before I left for London. You are not with child?"

"No, love. You left me happiness, nothing else."

Harry's world was rocking beneath his feet.

"Then tell me; I have the right to know. You gave me

your love-pledge. What has happened that you will not have me?"

She drew in a deep breath, steadying herself, lowering her eyes lest she should see the hurt in his own.

"When my mother lay sick of the sweating fever, she thought she was near to death. She told me things she thought I should know. It is not possible for us to wed, Harry."

"But *why?*"

At first, he had been afraid; now he was angry. What was there in the whole world, he thought, that could part them?

"Tell me," he urged, again.

"I cannot. I am ashamed enough. Once, there was a chance for us. Now there is none."

For an instant, Harry wanted to grasp the frail shoulders and shake the defiance out of her. He wanted to hit out at someone. Anyone. Beth loved him. Whatever she might say, her eyes betrayed her.

"Beth, sweetheart, you are pale and thin. You are not yourself. Come with me to Aldbridge. It is peaceful there, and you will soon be my Beth again."

"Dearest love." she took his hand and laid it to her cheek. "I have hurt you badly. I should have been more gentle with you. But you had to know. I had to tell you quickly, or I'd have been lost."

"You said you could not marry me, Beth, and I'll grant you must have your reasons. But can you, after all we have been to each other, tell me truly that you no longer love me?"

"No, Harry, I cannot say that; I shall love no one but you. *But I cannot marry you.*"

Desperately, he tried to understand. It didn't make sense. She loved him yet she would not marry him. Something had upset Beth. Something her mother had told her in a delirious fever.

Suddenly, he did not want to know the reason. Perhaps, he hazarded, if he could play for time, speak to Mistress Woodhall, there would be a way out of the nightmare? He lifted the latch of the door.

"I must speak with your mother" he said, urgently.

The bare room appalled him. In a corner on a straw palliasse, lay Beth's mother. By the cold empty hearth stood a single chair and on it plates, a mug and spoons. There was nothing else.

"Beth love, what is this?"

"We have sold the furniture," she said, simply.

"You have no money?"

She shook her head.

"I had to call a doctor and the apothecary needed payment. My mother needed milk."

The sleeping woman stirred then opened her eyes.

"Master Harry! You are welcome, young sir."

She held out her hand and bending down, Harry took it in his.

"I thank God you are home, safe."

"Are you well now, Mistress?"

"Aye, I thank you. I get stronger each day. Soon. I will be able to work again."

"But you cannot stay here!

"No, we cannot. It is only by the grace of the landlord that I lie here now. We owe rent money and there are but a few pence left for food. We must leave this house as soon as we are able."

"Can you travel, Mistress Woodhall? Can you make the journey to Aldbridge?"

"To Aldbridge?"

"Yes. You will be well cared for, there. You have been sick, and Beth is weak for lack of food. She talks nonsense, Mistress. She says she'll not wed me, now."

Sadly the woman shook her head.

"Would I had not told Beth. It was the ramblings of a woman close to death. I should have held my peace. I said it only because I wanted to cleanse my soul."

Harry placed his arm round the tired shoulders.

"Madam, it is clear to me that something is amiss, but it is also clear that you are both in no mood to talk straight. Come home with me. A week in the good sweet air and Agnes Muff's cooking will soon make you see things afresh. You were sick, Mistress. It is possible that you did not know what you said?"

"I know what I said, young Harry. I wish it had not been said. I wish with all my heart there had never been the need to say it." She shook her head sadly. "I would dearly like to come with you to Aldbridge. I could get strong and well there, I know."

"Then it is settled!" Triumphantly Harry turned to Beth. "You are coming home with me, love."

"No, Master Harry. Much as I would like it, we cannot accept your good offer. Not now. And what would your lady mother have to say about it?"

"My mother will have you, and gladly. I know it."

"It is a sore temptation." Jane Woodhall shook her head. "But after what has happened, it would be wrong to accept your hospitality."

"Nothing has happened, Mistress Woodhall." Harry would not be gainsaid. "Beth gave me her love-pledge. I intend to hold her to it."

"You cannot, Harry. You cannot; not when you know what I am!" Beth cried.

"I do not want to know, Beth. Not yet a while. When you are yourself again, when you are rested and strong, then we will talk."

Gently, he took her in his arms, stroking her long soft hair, feeling the frail bones beneath her thin dress.

"If you have ever loved me, Beth, come with me now. We will tell my father whatever it is that troubles you. He will know what to do. He is a good man, and wise. When you are rested, you can tell your worries to him. Only come with me?"

"Madam?"

Lost now to Harry's pleading and sick with longing for him, Beth appealed to her mother.

"There is nothing more I would like to do. To sleep in a soft bed; feel the warmth of a fire. And you, daughter. You have not eaten this last week. For just a little while, until I am able to work again, would it be so wrong?"

"Dearest Goody, please eat a little?"

Impatiently the old woman tossed her head.

"Leave me be, Anne. I am past food."

"But why will you not eat?" Anne set down the dish of syllabub. "Harry is home now, Goody, Home and safe. Why do you worry?"

"I am old, Anne Weaver. Old and tired."

Anne fussed with the rug that wrapped Goody's legs.

"Once, Goody, you said you'd not go to your Maker until you had placed Harry's first-born in his arms. Why are you sitting there, refusing food and willing death upon yourself?"

"Nay, Anne," Goody shook her head. "It's as if the life has already left me. Once, I hoped to place Harry's son in his arms. Now, I'm not so sure he'll ever get to the church door."

"He will, Goody. Oh, he will!" Gently Anne took the old hands in hers. "Listen to me and I will tell you something. This morning Harry set out for York with two horses. He means to bring his little Beth back with him, I'll wager!"

"And what if he does? You know as well as I that John is against the match."

"Well, *I'm* not, Goody Trewitt, so if you don't want to slip away to your Maker by the back door, you'd best keep up your strength."

But Goody could not be coaxed or comforted. Anne was stubborn and had a habit of getting her own way when she set her mind to it, but John had refused to be moved. Whenever Harry's marriage to Beth had been mentioned, he shut his mouth like a trap and would not even discuss it.

It was not like John, Goody told herself, to act like that. Why must he prevaricate so? Why wouldn't he talk

with the maid's parents? Whatever reason John had for
his actions, Goody knew he would not budge once his
mind had been made up. And what that reason was she
had no idea, but it plagued John mightily. John Weaver
was walking round these days like a bear with a sore
head, and that was certain.

Goody clucked impatiently as Anne settled a cushion
behind her head. It was only to be hoped, thought the
old midwife, that young Harry did not bring home his
little fancy, for if he did there would be nothing short
of an explosion in the house, what with John's moodiness
and Anne's stubbornness. If only, she sighed, they would
go away and leave her in peace.

It was pleasant to sit in the comfortable chair in the
sunlit window, waiting out her days. It was nice to be
fussed over, guarded anxiously, or sit by a fire she did
not even have to stir a finger to light, much less to mend.
Goody wanted nothing more of life than to be left in
peace with her memories, for her hopes were gone.

Anne drew up a chair and settled herself with her sewing. She would do better, she thought, to busy herself
with more gainful tasks. Usually, her sewing soothed her.
Today it irked her for she had already pricked herself
twice, so nervous were her fingers.

Soon it would be time for her to close for the winter
the airy room in which they sat. The solar was a pleasant
place, full of sunlight from the tall window that reached
from floor to ceiling. It was a pleasure to have her writing
chest and sewing table carried from the cosy winter-
parlour into the summer room, and wonder afresh at the

beauty of the blossom covered trees, and exult that winter was over.

Now those trees were laden with apples and pears, ready for gathering and storing. And when the fruit picking was done, they would know it was time to take down the hangings from the solar walls and sweeten them in the last of the summer sunshine before storing them away for the winter with lavender flowers in their folds.

And in the intimacy of the tiny parlour she would sit on cold winter nights, knitting, sewing fine linen shirts for John and Harry, or laboriously balancing her household accounts. Would she pass this coming winter with only her husband for company, or dare she hope, thought Anne, that there would be a little maid at her knee? Would she have Harry's wife by her side. How good it would be to have a daughter again.

Anne's mouth set in its stubborn line. Only let Harry bring his little maid home this day, and she would fight tooth and nail to keep her, aye, even if it meant defying her husband.

Both she and John were getting old. It was reasonable to want to see Harry settled and have the pleasure of grandchildren to fuss over. Only let me set eyes on this little wench, thought Anne, and I'll know at once if she's the one for Harry. And if she is, Anne vowed, I'll do all in my power to see them happy together.

Harry slowed his horse to a walking pace. They were nearing Aldbridge now, and he wanted the whole of the village to see his Beth. Bringing her home in this way, he thought, was the next best thing to announcing his betrothal from the church pulpit.

He glanced over his shoulder to where Mistress Woodhall wrapped in blankets, rode behind on the docile white mare. Fortified with meat and wine, she had made the journey well, and the soft warm air had coaxed a little colour into her wan cheeks.

Behind him, arms clasped around his waist, her cheek resting on his back, Beth had scarcely spoken since they had left York behind them.

"We are home now, sweetheart."

Harry felt the answering tremor of her body.

"You are not afraid, still, Beth?" ·

"I *am* afraid, Harry," she sighed. "Afraid I will grow to love your home and never want to leave its comfort again."

"So! I play second fiddle now to a great barn of a house?"

Harry's jocular words did not echo the hurt inside him. They had said little to each other during the journey, afraid lest the conversation should lead back to Beth's mysterious change of heart. She had been reluctant to come to Aldbridge. It had only been thoughts for her mother's welfare that had made her finally yield to Harry's insistent demands.

But once they had seen her, Harry knew his parents would love her; they would be captivated by her beauty and modesty. One shy glance from her wide blue eyes and his father would drop his opposition to their match, of that Harry was sure.

Cheerfully he acknowledged the greetings of the

villagers as they ran to their doors to watch them pass.

"Come and look at my Beth!" he wanted to shout. "Here is the maid who is to be my wife. Is she not most beautiful?"

"See it, over yonder, darling?" Harry pointed to where the old house stood encircled by trees of oak and beech. "Your new home!"

There was no reply from Beth who was seated so close to him and who was yet a million miles away.

John Weaver placed the basket of apples on the table and walked to the window-seat.

"I've been picking up windfalls," he said.

Anne's eyes did not lift from her sewing, although her fingers were still.

"I saw you from the window. Is it a fitting occupation for the master of the house, think you?"

Almost as though she had struck him, John's face registered pain. Anne had never acted like this before. Despite the position to which the Queen had thought fit to raise them, Anne had remained unchanged. She had accepted her new status as a challenge and the simple dignity with which she had always performed the tasks expected of her had quickly won her the respect of the villagers.

But always she had been *his* Anne, and when she was not being the lady of the manor it was her delight to run her fingers through a bowl of flour as though matching her skill as a pastry-cook with that of Agnes Muff.

That Anne should remind him that the owner of the Manor of Aldbridge should not stoop to pick up fallen apples would have seemed a joke had not her face been so serious.

"Anne love. What ails you? I have never heard you speak so proud before. Have you risen above the Anne I knew?"

"And have you forgotten, husband, the beloved man I once wed?"

"I don't understand you, Anne?"

"You forbid marriage to our son because he loves the daughter of a clerk, yet you grub amongst the orchard grass like a peasant! If you are determined to play the nobleman where your son's interests are at stake, then leave the work of the estate to the hired hands!"

"You do this to hurt me!"

"And what of me? And Harry and Beth?" Anne flung back. "Are you not hurting us?"

White-faced, John ran his fingers through his hair in a gesture of hopeless resignation. If only Anne could understand. But how could she understand if he did not tell her his reasons? Only that morning John had stood beneath Weaver's Oak, willing Meg back to him; talking to her with his heart.

"Meg, little love, help me?" he had silently pleaded.

And as he stood there, there had been a rustling in the leaves above his head and a feeling of peace had washed over him because it seemed then that Meg had heard him and understood his torment.

"Wait," the leaves had seemed to whisper.

Wait! thought John. Wait for what? For Harry to bring home his sweetheart; for Anne to range herself against him; for a miracle?

And then Anne's set face changed and the sewing slid from her lap to the polished boards beneath her feet. As though drawn by some invisible string she leaned closer to the window-glass, her face deathly white, her eyes dilated and unbelieving.

"Anne, dearest, what ails you?" John was at her side in an instant, his eyes following her agonized gaze.

Below them in the courtyard, Harry was helping a girl from his horse, his hands lingering for a moment on her slight waist. And then he pointed towards the house and she stood there, unsure and hesitant, her thin cloak moving in the breeze, her fair hair lifting and falling like gossamer about her.

John knew who she was; he had seen her before as she ran lightly across the Minster Yard. It shamed him now that he had not noticed what had instantly been obvious to Anne.

"Sweet Jesus," she whispered softly and covered her face with her hands as though not believing what she saw.

Then suddenly she dropped her fingers as though she expected the scene before her to have changed at second glance. Slowly she turned to John and her lips trembled to hide a sob whilst her eyes brimmed tears of happiness.

"Sweet Jesus, it is my Meg come back to me!"

And twenty years were gone in the blinking of an eyelid and Anne ran on feet that were light and young again to welcome her home.

In that instant of recognition John knew now that Anne would tolerate no interference. Now he knew he had no choice.

It seemed to Goody Trewitt that things were not as they should be.

John Weaver was agitated as a kitten on a hot grid-iron whilst Anne fussed over the little maid Harry had brought home. And if Mistress Woodhall apologised just once more for the commotion they were causing thought Goody, she'd have to start counting on her toes.

Place Harry's first-born in his arms? Why, she'd have to live as long as a donkey to do that! For a youngling in his prime and hot for his love, the lad seemed strangely subdued. And the little maid—there was an air of un-reality about her; a dreamy quality she had seen in Meg; a sadness about her eyes.

On the face of it, this was no love-match. Heaven help me, swore Goody, if this is what the modern generation call falling deep in love, then the day is not far short when midwives will go out of fashion!

She hunched her shawl about her shoulders and closed her eyes again. She wanted no part of it.

CHAPTER TWELVE

SAINTS help me, thought Anne Weaver, if I don't throw something! What with John sitting silent, Goody sulking and fasting and Harry and Beth acting like strangers, her patience was almost at an end.

Yesterday when she had first glimpsed Beth, Anne's happiness had been complete, for the years between seemed never to have been. The slight, fair girl who gazed in wonder at the grand house to which Harry had brought her might, for just a little time, have been Meg. Even yet, the likeness amazed and delighted Anne.

Harry was safe home from the wars and had brought his sweetheart to Aldbridge. Anne could not ask for more. Her heart had gone out to Beth at first sight. Had she chosen a wife for Harry herself, had she searched the length and breadth of the county, she could not have picked better. Now, Anne was beginning to realize, Beth was like Meg in more ways than in her looks.

It was becoming plain she had Meg's stubborn streak, for how else could she find it in her to refuse Harry? We'll see about that and all, Anne fumed. Beth Woodhall may not want Harry, but she had yet to reckon with My Lady, for My Lady was determined to have her for a daughter, no matter what.

If only John would help, Anne sighed. Surely he could see what a sweet little maid Harry had set his heart on? What reason could there now be, to forbid their marriage? Last night, John and Anne had lain in their big bed, wide-eyed yet each of them feigning sleep. Things had come to a pretty pass, Anne fretted, when husband and wife couldn't talk in the closeness of their bed.

And Harry—where was the spunk that had fought the Spaniards? What ailed him that he could accept the refusal of a slip of a girl? And why, after waiting so long *should* she refuse him? But Anne Weaver would not admit defeat. It seemed she stood alone.

John had withdrawn completely and Goody was indifferent. Harry wandered about bewildered and Beth was being stubborn. There was only Mistress Woodhall, Anne decided, to turn to. She liked Jane Woodhall. She was quiet and a little timid Anne thought, as if life had not dealt with her too kindly, poor deserted woman.

Mistress Woodhall had been appreciative of Anne's table and admiring of her beautiful home. She had taken the trouble to declare she had never slept in so soft and warm a bed, without waiting to be asked and had been pleased as a child when Anne had given her the blue silk dress with matching slippers.

"Are you sure you can spare them, Lady Anne," she had breathlessly asked, pirouetting before Anne's mirror. "I have never owned a fine gown—naught but fustian," she added wistfully.

It was natural, when they had eaten that day, to take her round the vast house. Proudly, like any other housewife, Anne went to great pains to show the prize that would come to the maid who married Harry Weaver.

They started in the garret rooms whose windows stood level with the tops of the great trees, and admired the heavy crop of fruit laid out in rows in the apple-room.

They passed through guest chambers, heavy with polished oak, that smelled faintly of beeswax and lavender flowers, their fat feather beds covered with heavy quilts of velvet.

They walked up staircases and down narrow passageways, poked into cupboards and store-chests and exclaimed together about the price of winter butter.

They peeped into the solar and the small cosy parlour and inspected the lofty kitchens.

"*Two* fireplaces, and only to *cook* on!" exclaimed Mistress Woodhall.

Agnes Muff and Molly liked her at once, for she remarked on the clean state of the floors, the fine array of pewter and the brightness of the copper ladles and skillets.

"We call this the great hall," said Anne, as they stepped into the vast room. "It is little used, for it is a barn of a place."

Her eyes indicated the high ceiling that stretched up into the roof of the house, criss-crossed with smoke blackened beams of curved oak. Lovingly her fingers traced out the coat of arms of the Weavers, newly carved and built into the massive oak fireplace. Anne had determined that it should be completed for Harry's return. It had been like an act of faith. And Harry had scarcely noticed it.

"Oh, but at Yule-tide we have such jollifications here, and then we are glad of this great room, for all the village visits us and there is such merry romping, I can tell you."

Anne glanced sideways at her companion.

"You would have such a fine time at Yule-tide, Mistress Woodhall, and the present giving at New Year. It would please me greatly to think you would still be with us for the festive season."

"And I would like it too, my lady." She shook her head sadly. "But I very much fear it will not be."

Anne clucked impatiently. She had had great hopes of Jane Woodhall's support—could she get help from no one?

She was not finished yet. Anne lit candles with a taper.

"Take heed of the steps, mistress," Anne warned as she opened the small door at the head of a flight of stone stairs. "They are worn for they are very old. This house was built on the foundations of a nunnery—the cellars were once the crypt."

Ranged before them, grostesque in the candlelight, was a row of great tun casks.

"This," said Anne, "is the Christmas ale, made special strong from the best barley; and this," she lovingly patted yet another towering barrel, "is Harry's wedding ale. We brewed it for him many years ago, and it is good and old now. 'Twill be a happy day for me when that cask is supped dry!"

Jane Woodhall's blue eyes misted over, but she remained silent. For all Anne's wiles, she could not draw one word of comfort from the woman's lips.

"Lady Anne," impulsively she spoke at last, "you are so kind and good and I fear we were wrong to have accepted your hospitality. We should not have come here, knowing all along it could come to nothing."

"*Need* it come to nothing?" asked Anne.

"I fear so, and I blame myself. Would I had not told Beth."

Wisely, Anne held her peace. Soon, if she were careful, they would start to get at the truth of the mystery.

"I was sick of the sweating fever and near I thought, to dying," Jane Woodhall rushed on. "There were things I thought Beth should know about herself. Foolishly, I told her before I begged for the priest."

There were tears now in the woman's eyes and Anne's warm heart leaned out to her.

"I would be so happy, my lady, and so proud for my Beth to live in this beautiful place. And you, madam, are so good, for all your grand position."

"Position?" Anne threw back her head and laughed. "Do you know, Mistress Jane, that once I worked in this grand house as a servant? There is not one corner of it I have not cleansed or polished. When Sir Crispin Wakeman lived here, I was no grand lady, I can tell you!"

"Sir Crispin Wakeman?" whispered Jane Woodhall.

"Aye. He fled the country after the uprising. The Queen saw fit then to give this manor to my John. Why do you ask?"

"I ask it because—" She drew a shuddering breath. "My lady, is there some place private where we can talk? I'll swear I can hold my peace no longer. You have been kind to us and it is right you should know. And if it please you, I'd like fine if Sir John can hear what I have to say, and all."

Anne placed her arms round the trembling shoulders.

"It is bright and warm in the solar. Come," she said, "let us find my husband."

Anne closed the door firmly behind her and settled herself on the stool by John's chair.

"Now, mistress?" she prompted, kindly.

Hesitantly, the woman looked around her.

"We shall not be disturbed?" she faltered. "The younglings . . . ?"

"They are walking together, outside," supplied Anne, "and a good thing, too!"

She said it with more hope than conviction.

"Get you gone into the gardens!" she had hissed to Harry. "Do you want your mother to do your courting for you?"

"And Mistress Goody?" Jane Woodhall nodded to where the old woman dozed by the window.

"She will not trouble us," replied Anne. "She just prays and sleeps. Today, I tried to tempt her with chicken legs and a dish of syllabub, but it was all to no avail. I fear that when Goody Trewitt refuses her victuals, something is sadly wrong."

"Sir John. My lady," Jane Woodhall hesitated. "I beg your pardon for the trouble we have caused you. When you have heard what I have to tell you, I pray you will understand that we must be on our way."

"I am sorry, mistress." For the first time, John spoke. "I am truly sorry that it should come to this. I think I know what you are about to tell us."

"John?"

Anne reached instinctively for her husband's hand. She sensed now that soon she would know what had been troubling her man for so long, and it rippled fear to the tips of her toes.

"Then bear with me, Sir John, for I am near to heart-break." Jane Woodhall drew a deep, steadying breath. "You remember the uprising near on twenty years ago?"

"I should. Oh, I should!"

"It caused me grief and all, my lady. I was a dairy-maid in Warwickshire and love-pledged to my master's ploughman. We were to be wed at Yule-tide, and none happier than we two. But the earls from the north rose up for Mary Stuart and Peter, my man, was true to the old faith. He followed them and was taken prisoner to London."

She stared for a moment into the hearth.

"I was near demented, for I loved him with all my heart. There was nowhere then for me to go—I had no kin—and my master had fled. He too, was a Catholic and feared for his life."

"They were terrible times, Mistress Jane," whispered Anne.

"Aye," she nodded. "Since there was no one to care what I did, I trudged to London, looking for Peter. I found he had been thrown into prison with many more, but I managed to get word to him. A pretty wench can charm even the hardest gaoler, if she sets her mind to it."

"I understand," Anne said.

"My Peter was a fine man, and a good one. I think in time he would have been pardoned. Many were, but not

Peter. When a man's hair is the colour of the devil's, he is marked."

"The devil's hair, mistress?" John was bemused. "What colour *is* the devil's hair?"

"It is the colour of the red leaves of autumn. Peter's hair was red, and it was his undoing. Strange, for I loved to twine his curls about my fingers."

"Red hair?"

Anne felt a shock of pain. Somewhere, in the background of her mind, a warning sounded. Unlike her, John was quite calm. Anne had felt no reaction from his hand, no indication that the mention of red hair had caused him unease. But John was calm because he knew, didn't he? And soon the pieces would fit together and she would know, too.

"Aye, Master Harry has it, too. Oh, my lady, I mean no disrespect to the lad" she hastened, flushing, for she was saying all the wrong things, she knew.

"Go on." John helped with a smile.

"Well, Sir John, Peter broke loose with a score of prisoners, but he was soon taken again. When he told them his name they would not believe him. 'You are no ploughman!' they mocked him. 'Do you think you can save your treacherous hide by adding lies to treason?' They thought he was another—a richer prize. They thought he was a nobleman's son, and so he died."

She wiped a tear from her cheek with the back of a trembling hand.

"At least he died a gentleman and quick, by the axe," she whispered.

"And this nobleman's son?"

"*Nobleman?* My lady, you will not believe this, but Fate plays strange tricks. I was walking the London taverns, trying to find a man who would give me the price of food and a bed, and I came upon this nobleman. At first I thought it was Peter and I ran to him, scarce able to believe my eyes. And then I saw I had been mistaken. There was a likeness, you see. 'You are the nobleman they seek,' I accused him. 'My Peter died in your place.' I threatened to denounce him and he offered me money, but I wanted more than money. The price of my silence was wedlock!"

"And he married you?"

"Aye, Lady Anne. Master Cedric Woodhall married me, and we came to York. Try as I would, I could not find at first what his true name was. Then, one night, when Beth was still a little thing, he came home the worse for wine, and I knew. He mocked me and told me I was a slut of a dairymaid and that he'd have rid of me when the true Queen of England came into her own."

"He was a terrible man. Your life must have been most unhappy." Anne sympathised, willing her to go on.

"He was a traitor and a spy. That I also learned from his drunken stupor. He had offered his services to Sir Francis Walsingham. He spied for Walsingham against his own faith. But he never gave up the old religion and his conscience and ambition wouldn't let him rest. As long as Mary Stuart lived, there was hope for him, he thought. It wasn't so much the old faith he worried about. All he wanted was his estates back, and revenge. Woodhall turned traitor to Queen Elizabeth, and played a double game; spying for Walsingham and at the same time aiding Catholic priests. He boasted about it. He told me if I ever repeated a word of what he'd said, he'd slit my throat and throw me in the Ouse."

There was a small silence, broken only by the spitting of birch logs.

"One day he said he'd have his birthright restored to him and then Beth would marry into her true station and I could go to the devil." She gave a little laugh. "The devil? I'd lived with him for years! There was no love lost between us. Even at Beth's christening we glowered hatred at each other across the font. 'We'll call the babe for the Queen,' I said, and when the priest asked 'Name this child?' I answered 'Elizabeth' and *he* said 'Mary', for the Stuart. So the bewildered priest christened her Elizabeth Mary, for two queens. My husband would never use the name, Elizabeth. Beth, he always called her."

"You *never* loved him, mistress?"

"Never!" she replied with conviction. "I allowed him into my bed but once." She shrugged. "I had to," she said, simply.

"I grieve for you, Mistress Woodhall," Anne said, reaching out for the thin agitated hand.

"Mistress *Woodhall*—there's the laugh! Do you know what I found my real name to be, my lady? Oh, it was strange to hear you mention it in the cellars."

"I?" questioned Anne.

"Yes, my lady. Once, you said, you worked for him— Sir Crispin Wakeman. I married Kit, his son."

"You married . . . *Kit Wakeman?*"

Anne's voice came in a strangled whisper. Desperately

John squeezed her hand in his own. The truth was out, now. He knew from the stricken look in Anne's eyes that she had instantly grasped the implication of Jane Woodhall's words.

Panic stricken, Anne turned to John.

"Kit Wakeman is dead. You saw his head, you told me, on London Bridge!"

"I thought I had done, Anne. The hair was the same colour. Believe me, I thought truly he had died."

"It was my Peter who died. So I married the traitor who let him go to his death, and spent the rest of my life hating him. Now, I have only one fear. I pray he will never return to us, for I would rather sew and scrub for the rest of my days than live with that black-hearted man again."

Anne did not clearly hear the words Jane Woodhall spoke so bitterly. Somewhere, they echoed above her head, then drifted into Eternity where all echoes go. And Mary Stuart, damn her, was back from Eternity to enjoy the fresh heartbreak she was causing.

John had known all along Anne realised. She had not trusted him. She had accused him of being unjust and of rising above himself, yet all the time he had been trying to spare her. And what of Harry who loved Beth so dearly? And what of Beth who loved Harry? Was Harry to be told of this? "You cannot marry Beth Woodhall, for it is forbidden to bed your own sister!"

Perhaps, in time, he would understand, but would he ever forgive them? Would he blame them for not telling him the truth about himself? Desperately, she tried to bring herself to speak.

"You say you pray he will not return. Where is he now?"

"I don't know, Lady Anne. I think things must have got too hot for him, and he skipped the country. I hope with all my heart he will never come back."

"There is little fear of that, Mistress Jane, now that Philip's Armada has been defeated." John gave a little sad smile. "Does it not seem strange to you that this house in which we sit might one day have been yours?"

"Mine, Sir John?"

"It is almost certain Kit Wakeman would have had his estates restored to him if Mary Stuart had taken Elizabeth Tudor's throne."

"He'd have had rid of me—he made that quite plain."

Desperately, Anne clung to John's hand, willing herself back to normality, knowing what must be done yet dreading having to do it. First it had been Meg. Now it was Harry's turn to know heartbreak. Mary Stuart's echo mocked her as she struggled to her feet.

"I think, John, I would like a sup of cool water. Will you ring the bell for Molly?"

Suddenly the simple act of lifting the silver bell seemed too much for Anne. Bitterly she glanced into the window seat where Goody dozed her life away. Wise old woman, to want to leave this world of sadness. Dear Goody Trewitt. She would never live long enough now, even had she wanted it, to see the birth of Harry's children.

Do you want your mother to do your courting for you? Anne had chided Harry.

"Sweet Jesus," she prayed, "where will it all end?"
Presently she spoke.

"Who's to tell Harry?"

"I think Beth will tell him," Jane Woodhall replied
gently. "But I am glad, for all that, I have eased my sins
from my soul. It was a wicked thing I did. Would I had
not done it. There is much, though, a woman will do to
save her child from the taint of bastardy."

"Bastardy, mistress? I don't think you can call Beth a
bastard. She was fathered in wedlock. And anyway it is
no shame on her if she were one, to my way of thinking."

In defending Beth, she knew, Anne was defending
Harry.

"She *is* one, and there *is* shame on it. Shame at least if
you are poor. Why, even you seem to agree now that
Harry and Beth should not marry. The daughter of a
clerk maybe, could have risen one day to take her place
amongst the nobility. But a ploughman's bastard . . . "

"Mistress Jane, what are you saying? A *ploughman's*
bastard?"

"Did you not understand me rightly? I thought I had
made myself plain. I told Beth who her true father was
because I thought I was near to death. The swine I
married couldn't have claimed her then, had he
returned. Beth had no love for him, even though she
believed him to be her father. Little did I think she
should feel shame and refuse to marry Harry, because
of it."

John rubbed the back of his neck with his hand. Somewhere in the midst of his bemusement, there was a ray
of hope.

"Are you trying to tell us that Kit Wakeman did not father Beth?"

"I thought I *had* told you. When I was in London, I realised I was carrying Peter's child in me. Beth was, I suppose, Peter's last gift to me before he went to fight for Mary Stuart. I had to get my babe fathered. That's why I had to bed with the man I married. He had to believe Beth was his own, and once was enough to do it. Beth was frail, as an infant. He believed me when I said she had been born before her time." She shrugged. "Anyway, why shouldn't he support my child? Had it not been for him letting Peter die in his place, there'd have been no need for it. It was rough justice, I suppose. Only I was the one to suffer from it!"

Molly entered the room and bobbed a curtsey. "My lady?"

"Bring water for Lady Anne?" John asked.

"No, Molly!" Suddenly Anne was smiling. "I have a taste for wine. In the cellar there is a bottle of Spanish wine. Carry it carefully and polish the best goblets, Molly. I have a mind to drink a toast!"

"Gently, Anne," John cautioned. "Beth has said she'll not have Harry."

"Not have Harry? We'll see about that!"

Suddenly Anne was light-hearted.

"Mistress Woodhall, I have a fancy to see our son wed to your little Beth. Do you think that between us we could persuade her?"

"You mean, my lady, you are willing they should wed, in spite of what I have told you?"

"In spite of—*because* of, maybe. Mistress, why should

our children suffer for our mistakes? I love your little maid. I want her for my daughter. We *both* want her for our daughter."

Smiling, Anne held out her hand to John and smiling, he took it in his own.

"That we do, Mistress Jane."

Wait, Meg had whispered. Meg had had faith.

"Then what's to be done? Beth can be mortal stubborn when she sets her mind to it. She feels the shame of her parentage badly."

"Shame? Where's the shame?" Goody Trewitt opened her eyes.

"Goody! You've been listening to every word we said."

The laughter in Anne's eyes belied the severity in her voice.

"What if I have, Anne Weaver? And if you'll take the advice of an old woman, you'll whip that maid into obedience! Or maybe," she glanced slyly through the window, "young Harry's done it already!"

She pointed to where Beth and Harry stood.

"Over yonder—by the white rose bush."

They were standing close together, heads bent, so near that their toes were touching. Gently Harry took Beth's face in his hands and she did not resist when he kissed her lips. Then her arms were round him pulling him closer to her and she offered her lips to him, returning his kisses with an ardour that matched his own.

"I think, Mistress Jane, he has kissed away her shame," Anne sniffed through her tears.

"I think my Lady Weaver, you may well be right."

Jane accepted the flimsy lace 'kerchief Anne offered, and blew her nose noisily. And John said nothing, but the smile that spread across his face lighted his eyes with happiness for it was of the pure gold of contentment.

"Oh, you make a fine picture the three of you, grinning and weeping," Goody grumbled. "Nobody cares about an old woman that hasn't eaten a square meal in months!"

"Goody," breathed Anne. "You mentioned *food?*"

"I did, Anne Weaver. What else would a body talk about when she's hungry? Chicken legs, you said? How am I to keep up my strength with my belly rumbling from lack of sustenance?"

She glanced again through the window to where the lovers were locked away, still, in their own little world and started to make a mental calculation.

"How soon can you get them to the church, Anne? A week, you reckon?"

"A week, Mistress Woodhall?" Anne enquired.

"I think a week will do nicely, my lady."

"Now, let's see—" Goody resumed her counting. "A week to the church; a couple of months to prove his manhood; that should make it . . . " Goody reckoned on her fingers. " . . . that should make it about the end of next August!"

She looked up, suddenly smiling.

"Yes, I think I can keep this old body together for another twelve-month. Well, Anne Weaver, what are you waiting for? I want my chicken legs!"

"Yes, Goody. Oh, yes!" Anne breathed.

"And a bowl of syllabub to follow," the old midwife called to the echo of Anne's happy feet. "A *large* bowl of syllabub!"

POSTSCRIPT

ALDBRIDGE still stands on the sweet Plain of York though the traveller may not recognise it at first, for now it bears another name.

The roofs of the manor house and St. Olave's church stand sentinel yet over the village, though there is no trace of the oak that John Weaver planted.

It is said thereabouts that those who stand at the crossroads on a summer's evening may sense a sighing on the breeze, but none will admit to hearing it, for Yorkshiremen are taciturn folk and wary of strangers.

The verger of St. Olave's may, if he takes a liking to the enquirer, carefully open the old parish registers. He will show Father Sowerbye's spidery writing faded brown on yellowed pages recording that

On the seventh day of September, A.D. 1589, were the twin children of Elizabeth Mary and Harry Weaver carried to this church and christened Diccon and Meg.

It may be found also that in that same year,

On Childermas Eve, did Mistress Gudrun Trewitt, goodwife of this parish, die quiet in her sleep and was laid peacefully to rest on the last day of December.

If you should discover Aldbridge, tread carefully, for the heartsease grows there still.